JANE BOND
DARK SIDE OF
THE MOON

V.R. Tapscott

Thanks to:
My wife, as per usual.
My beta readers, again, as per usual. My books would take a lot longer to write if I didn't have outstanding beta readers to help with the details.
My friend Kris, who offered valuable insights!
Seth Deitrich ("TW Griffith", and "Ambush", available on Amazon) for technical details regarding cops and military.
My friend Jax, who really taught me how to write. And, once again, showed me that pain and suffering make great stories. The good times – not so much.
Any wrong details in the book are on me, not on any of the people above.

CONTENTS

CHAPTER ONE

Starting Up.

After a month or so of Kit being gone, I started feeling like maybe it was time to explore the basement a bit more.

Dale had stayed for almost the entire time and we'd gotten close, sharing walks and time at the Lake. Finally, though, his vacation had run out and he had gone back to Montana. He'd checked out the local ranger district and thought he could get on, and we've progressed to the point of both of us liking the idea that he could relocate here.

So, here I was, standing at the bottom of the stairs below the house. Dale and I had hauled various furniture down here to make the "scenery room" feel a bit more homey. I'd spent many hours down here just lying back in the recliner and enjoying the ambience. But, this time of year, the outside called and since it's definitely a situation of this room being here for a long time, but nice days outside were limited - we'd spent that time outside. Today promised to be a real scorcher. This week and most of the next, the temps were expected to be over 100, so a good week to spend inside.

I walked through the tropical rain forest that was today's display. I usually just let it randomize unless I have something specific in mind. I don't know where it pulls these pictures from, but some of the leaves on some of the trees don't even seem to be trees from earth. Of course, things change a lot and they could be from prehistory, or they could be a very advanced and

4

sophisticated CGI display. In the end, it's soothing and relaxing and I don't really care much how it gets there. Call me a pragmatist, I guess.

Kit had left me some things and in the aftermath of him leaving, having Dale here, and everything else going on I'd not had the time - or the heart - to look at them. Today seemed like a good day for the hunt, though.

I spent the afternoon wandering around the area underneath my barn. It's really huge, I may have to find a way to make it into a garage or something. This much perfectly dry and perfectly indestructible area should be utilized for a useful purpose rather than a monument - or mausoleum - for Kit.

I finally stopped walking aimlessly and went over and sat in the flyer, which I still had no idea how to make it fly or how to get it out of the basement even if I did. I looked around, discouraged. The seats were even plastic, Kit had probably made them like that as a joke since it was something we argued about.

I sighed and said, "Kit, I miss you."

A voice came from the speaker grille. "Voice print check pass. Retinal scan pass. Command sequence accepted. System initializing."

I sat up straight. "Kit??"

Nothing. All was silent and I was beginning to think I'd dropped off and dreamed it, when the voice came back. "All systems fully functional. Power at full capacity. AI integrity check pass. Good afternoon, Jane Bond. What may I assist you with?"

"Kit? Is that you? I thought you were gone!"

In a stilted machine voice, "Jane Bond, I am a Mark VI Survey Class AI. I am currently running in Initialize mode. Contact has not been established with the Command Module, however all systems are nominal. I have been programmed to carry out whatever orders are given me by Jane Bond. What are your wishes?"

I started to breathe again. "What is your name, I can't call you AI Pilot."

"Why can you not call me AI Pilot?"

5

"Well, it wouldn't be polite. Did Kit teach you about the internet?"

"The previous Mark V Survey Class AI did an upload of data to my storage system. Do you authorize access to this database?"

I blinked. "Um, yes, of course I authorize access."

"Access acquired, one moment please."

After considerably longer than one moment, the voice came again. "Full system reinitialization instituted, this will take several minutes. Have a nice day."

I sat for a while, looking dumbly at the console. How in the world had I started a "full system initialization" and what WAS that anyhow? It didn't sound very reassuring, and the minutes stretched on. Finally, I gave up and went over and sat in one of the chairs and watched the display, but even that wasn't very relaxing as it was showing some sort of volcanic activity with all kinds of things being blown up or melted. Probably reflecting my mindset - I shivered, thinking I'd probably managed to ruin whatever Kit had left for me.

I must have dozed, since I jerked awake to that voice again. "Jane Bond, I am a Mark VI Survey Class AI. I am currently running in Pilot mode. Contact has not been established with the Command Module. Pilot Module 'Olive' being brought on line. Please wait."

I'd just dropped off to sleep when a plaintive little voice came.

"Hello? Is anyone there?"

I jumped up, thinking someone must have come down the stairs from the barn. I always lock that and hide it, but I've missed it a couple times. I reached the bottom of the stairs and no one was there, and the door at the top was closed tight.

I was standing there considering psychiatric options when the voice came again.

"Hello? It's scary down here, is there someone there?"

It sounded like a girl about twelve years old. Finally, I said "Hello?" figuring I'd triangulate on the voice and find her when she spoke again.

Immediately it came back and said "Oh, hello! I'm so happy there's someone here! I'm Olive, are you Jane?"

The voice was coming from the ship.

I said "Yes, I'm Jane. Are you ... um ... the ship?"

The voice came back with a smile in it, and somehow sounded older and more confident. "No, I'm the Pilot Module but I'm not the ship. It is a very nice ship though, I can see it was built by my predecessor. You called him Kit. He was very smart and left me lots and lots of notes. Lots. And lots. They're not very well organized though. He was insane, so I suppose that might have something to do with it."

I blinked. "Kit was very nice. He was my friend."

The voice grew a little pensive. "Oh, yes, I'm sure he was very nice, and he was your friend, but he was still insane. Not that there's anything wrong with that, many nice people have been insane. You should be happy to know that the Mark VI has been re-engineered to be nearly insanity proof!"

Wryly, "Yes, I feel much better."

"I know, right? I still have to make sure I do self-checks and the like, but so far so good! Did I mention my name is Olive? Kit left a note that you'd like to give me a name, I hope it's all right that I picked one out already?"

I could feel my eyebrows reaching for the sky. "No, that's fine, Olive. And it's very nice to meet you." I made my way up the ramp and sat down in the ship.

"Do you pilot the ship like Kit did?"

Just a tiny bit of snark, "No, I don't blow things up and crash." A pause, then, "Sorry. That wasn't very nice. And yes, I can pilot the ship. I have all the notes and ... um ... "

"You don't know how to pilot the ship?"

"Of course I know how to pilot the ship!" With that, the ship rose off the ground and hit the ceiling with a solid whack.

"Olive! What are you doing?"

"I'm piloting the ship! What do you think?"

"I think you're hitting the ceiling of the garage and you're gonna break something!"

In a chagrined tone of voice, "Oh. Well. I didn't know that was there. Hang on ... "

After a couple minutes of hanging there in the air, pressed up against the ceiling, it suddenly vanished, and the ship popped out into the sunshine. And then, Olive yelled "Yahoo!!" and we took off up into the sky at about a million miles an hour. We went through a flock of seagulls and Lucy. You know, the one with diamonds. I sat there, petrified, while the sky got bluer and bluer.

Pretty soon I yelled, "Olive, the air's getting thin out here and I need to breathe!"

"Oh, sorry, I'm a little busy. Um. Hang on."

I wasn't very happy about "hang on" when I was starting to have a harder and harder time breathing. Pretty soon though, I could see a difference in the shade of the light, and it got easier to take a breath again.

After a little bit longer, a slightly frantic voice, "I have no idea how to stop! Sorry. Going through notes."

The ship really seemed to hit its stride after we rammed through the top of the atmosphere and I sat on my hands to keep from chewing my nails off as we rocketed toward the moon. As we got closer, I started eyeing various places in the Sea of Tranquility wondering if any of them were softer than others.

Just about the time I decided I'd be seeing Neil Armstrong's footyprints up close and personal, we slammed to a stop. I mean, a dead stop. Instantly. It was weird.

Olive said, "Hey, I found the controls to stop!"

I swallowed. "I see that. Is that the Apollo 11 Lunar Module over there?" I pointed out the window to the left.

Indifferently. "Yeah, I guess so. Want to see it closer?"

Without waiting she whisked over next to the spacecraft and I took a good look, snapping a few shots with my phone. My mouth was still a little dry at the thought of us stopping about ten feet short of making another crater in the moon. A big one.

I swallowed again. "I thought you couldn't leave the planet surface."

Olive laughed. "Yeah, Kit couldn't, but that was because he wasn't a Command Module and didn't have one accessible. I AM the Command Module, so I can go anywhere I want."

She seemed to think about this statement for a minute. "Um, well, I guess anywhere you want."

She suddenly sounded anxious. "I didn't mean to scare the crap out of you, Jane. It was just so neat being free."

I sighed and smiled. "Olive, I know that's how you feel. But be careful of those thoughts. Kit wasn't really so much insane as uncaring about life. It worried me when you thoughtlessly headed into space, completely forgetting it would kill me.

A tiny voice, "I'm sorry, Jane. Should I re-initialize and restart my program? Try a different Olive?"

I blinked. "What? Oh, my no, Olive. I like you, and besides we don't just throw a friend overboard when she makes a mistake. Even after all that happened, Kit was my friend - Kit IS my friend. I made sure Celeste promised she wasn't going to wipe him. Just ... you know, ask me before you try to kill me!"

"Oh, I would never ... um. I guess I just about did, didn't I?"

"Yeah, kinda." She was silent for several beats.

"Um, Jane?

"Uh huh, Olive?"

"You want to explore a little on the moon?"

"Now that sounds like fun! Let me get my skinsuit on!" I pulled it out of the closet and slid into it. I heard Olive's intake of breath."

"Jane?"

"Hm?"

"What is that thing?"

I frowned. "It's my skinsuit, why?"

With a disapproving sound to her voice she said, "Well, it's certainly a SKINsuit, all right. Let me guess, Kit designed it?"

I said, "Well, I guess. I thought it was just how they were made. It is ... a little embarrassing to wear in public."

"I can certainly see THAT. I'm blushing for you just looking at it."

"Hey, it saved my life a lot of times!"

In a huffy voice she said, "Put it back in the closet."

"What? I want to explore!"

"I'll make you a new one, Jane. Just put that ... thing ... back in the closet."

I hung it back in the closet and stood there, naked, in the ship. Thank goodness it was warm! "Hey, don't waste time, I need some clothes and I don't want to have to change again."

"Jane, you rush a miracle, you get a bad miracle."

I paced around the tiny ship, and pretty soon I swear I heard a "Ding!" in the closet.

"Ok, it's ready."

I opened the closet and pulled out the new suit. It was still scandalously tight, but this one had leggings like yoga pants, and a real shirt like a tight tee shirt. I put it on and it fit just like the other one, but I felt more like I was dressed. It also had pockets and even a Batman-style utility belt!

In an excited tone of voice, Olive said, "Put up the hood!"

I was still getting used to the hood, since even though I knew its usefulness I hated having it up since it made me look like an Area 51 refugee. "Hood up."

Nothing happened.

"Um, Olive, something's wrong, the hood isn't working."

She giggled. "Yeah, it is."

"No, it's not. I can see my reflection and it's not there."

She laughed. "It is too! Kit was quite the jokester, wasn't he?"

I frowned. "You mean it's invisible?"

I could hear the smirk in her voice. "Yup."

I was slightly outraged. "You mean I've been wearing this naked suit with the google eyed helmet all this time and it could have been different??"

Her mirth faded. "Um, yeah. I could make you a suit that looks like Oprah Winfrey, but I think you're cute and sexy how you are. So, I made a Jane suit. See?"

"With an invisible helmet."

"Yup. You look perfect just how you are, Jane."

I rolled my eyes. "Don't pour it on too thick, Miss AI. You don't have that much to make up for.

Her voice became very serious. "I do, Jane. I'd not exist except for you. And for that matter ... " She went silent for a bit, then, "Jane, I swear to you that I'll always do my best for you, and to keep you safe and never lie to you or do anything to harm you or to allow harm to come to you."

This time I swallowed a lump. "Thank you, Olive. I'll try really hard to deserve you."

"Me too, Jane. Me too." Then the mirth returned to her voice. "Only, I reserve the right to laugh at your bad hair days and wardrobe choices!"

I wasn't sure what vacuum would do to my camera, so I got Olive to make me a clear case for my phone. It looked just like my phone, but she assured me it was now vacuum-proof and waterproof. Knowing the technology, it was probably volcano and mountain lion-proof as well, although I didn't intend to push it to find out. Once I was ready, we moved to an area of the moon that didn't show up on the telescopes and I bounded about, taking pictures and grabbing a few moon rocks of my own to take back in the multitude of pockets. I was brought back to earth with a thump by my phone vibrating and the alarm pop up.

"Ohmigosh, Olive! I'm supposed to be home! The girls and I had a swim party planned for tonight and as usual I forgot and they're waiting for rides!"

Olive zipped the flyer over and I jumped in, and we set off for home. About halfway back to the earth, I said casually, "Sure nice to be invisible - I'd hate for NORAD to try to shoot us down."

"Invisible?"

"Uh huh. You know, the ship is invisible so we can't be ... Olive? We ARE invisible, right?"

"How mad would you be if I said, 'No'?"

"I wouldn't be mad. I'd just say, 'Get the invisibility up, pronto!'"

"In that case, NO. And I'm working on it."

"Well, don't waste time!"

"Then stop TALKING to me. It takes processor cycles to talk!"

I fell silent, and waited, and as we got closer, I thought about all the news stories there'd be about the weird reverse meteor that flew up OUT of Chelan earlier today. I hoped I wouldn't read any stories about an incoming one later. Then I had an internal groan - there were probably pictures someplace of me pacing naked inside the ship - in the middle of the freekin' Sea of Tranquility! Maybe no one was watching ...

My phone vibrated. I answered it.

"Hello, mother. Uh huh, I'm fine. The moon? What are you talking about? Of course not, how would I get to the moon? Lunch? Um, maybe. I'll call?"

I glared at my phone. She'd hung up on me!

"OLIVE! We need to be invisible RIGHT NOW!"

"Yeah, yeah, hang on, I'm working on it."

"That was my mother. She has pictures, but apparently, they're not quite good enough to really identify me. On the moon. Pacing. Naked."

"How does your mother have pictures of the moon?"

I heaved a long sigh. "She's high level military. They probably have a platoon of spy satellites watching the moon in case of some sort of invasion."

"Invasion. From the MOON?" She broke into laughter. "The MOON? Tell her to watch Pluto, not the MOON."

I eyed the display. "Are you serious?"

She giggled. "No, not really. I think they're asleep out there. A complete regen takes a LONG time. We probably won't hear from them for years."

"Oh." Suddenly I felt a little sad. Kit was out there, asleep ... getting psycho shrunk or whatever they do to a crazy computer.

Olive said softly, "Hey. I know I'm not Kit, but do you want to talk about it?"

I wiped my eyes and waved my hands around. "No, I'm fine. Just, he's my friend and I worry. How are we doing on the invisible thing?"

"Oh, I got that taken care of. Like ... thousands of milliseconds ago. In fact, look outside."

I sniffed, blinked and looked out the window. We were back inside the garage again. "Wow, nice job, Olive!" I glanced at my watch; I'd still almost have time. I bolted for the stairs and up into the barn - started up Threepio and tootled off. I'd almost gotten out the driveway when I realized there was a tiny light hovering near my rearview mirror.

"Olive?"

Her voice was a little nervous sounding, "Okay if I come along?"

"Sure, just make sure you don't show yourself, my friends don't know about Kit or any of my more extracurricular activities." She popped through the glass and nestled into the front of the sun-visor, I suppose so she could see out. Kit's original bottle was incorporated into Threepio, so Olive was able to have a presence here.

"Olive, in case you don't have any records of it, Kit and I kind of worked out a deal where he'd mostly stay out of my head unless it was an emergency. It's pretty hard to pay attention to people around you when the voices in your head are so loud." I smiled, "So, usually he spoke through the radio speaker or through my cell phone speaker, plus it also looks a little better from the outside to be talking on a phone than warbling to yourself as you tool through the Walmart parking lot."

The radio speaker came to life and Olive's voice came, "Gotcha boss, I'll be quiet." She had a warm voice that I liked immediately, kind of a not-quite Southern drawl.

We drove around the perimeter of the town and stopped at Bailey's condo, or more accurately we stopped in front of Bailey, who was sitting on the curb with her purse between her feet and an irritated look on her face. She came around the driver's side and popped the door open. I knew what was coming and unbuckled my seatbelt. She grabbed me and pulled me out in the middle of the road and gave me a big hug.

"Hey, I missed you - having Dale here was like not having YOU here at all."

I blushed a little. "I guess we did a lot of stuff together, and I wound up doing most of my workouts at home."

She grinned. "Yeah, I bet.

I blushed again, and this time just didn't say anything.

With a self-satisfied grin, she went around to the passenger side and got in. Bailey has this arcane method of choosing whether she sits in front or back, and apparently today was shotgun day, since she sat in the front.

"So, why are you late TODAY? You always have such interesting explanations that sound so much like lies I wonder if they're the truth. Last time I think it was Australia. What about today?"

"Oh, I was on the moon. I popped up there and ran around for a while, gathered some rocks." I scrabbled in one of my numerous pockets and brought out a rock. "Here, one for you."

She rolled her eyes as she glanced at it, took a closer look and frowned at me, then put it in her purse and didn't say another word about it. "I see you got some new workout clothes. It looks pretty slinky - where did you get that?"

Now, I'd almost forgotten that I'd been in so much of a hurry I didn't change out of my skinsuit. But Bailey was right, it was a pretty good-looking workout set, so I went with that. "Yeah, I picked that up on the moon too."

"Mmhmm, nice gym up there? Lululemon opened a shop?"

"Something like that. I got a discount since it was only a half-moon."

She snorted. "Yeah, I think you topped me." She frowned as she got a closer look. "It's all one piece - even has gloves." She leaned over and looked. "And yeah, it's got boots too." She looked closer. "They're not boots either, some kind of toe socks? I've never seen workout clothes like those."

I shifted a little uncomfortably. "It's a new one, I got a chance to try it out through the school - I still get mailings from there."

She looked at me speculatively. "It's something to do with the thing that happened last year that you won't tell me about, isn't it?" She dug the moon rock back out of her purse and looked at it. "I bet if I had this tested, I'd find out it really IS moon rock."

I whined, "Baaailley ... "

She smirked. "Ok, I'll let it drop, but you HAVE to tell me about it someday."

I patted her arm and said, "I promise."

She said, "Okay. And that was weird 'cause it felt like fingers when you touched me, it definitely didn't feel like gloves. But I'm dropping it. Really."

I forged ahead, "So, how has your summer gone, dearie? It's getting hot out and we haven't had a chance to have even one decadent day in the sun, yet!"

She dropped back in the seat. "I don't know, it's always something. There's some kind of buyout on the table at the magazine, so here pretty soon I may wind up with lots of money and no job.

"Is that good news or bad?"

"I don't really know. It could go either way, I suppose. It's enough money I could simply retire, but I like what I do. I'd probably need to find another job to at least keep my hand in. "

Offhandedly, I said, "You could take care of the office and run Bond Investigations, I guess."

Bailey made and excited wiggle. "Bond Investigations? Is it official, you're gonna hang out a shingle?

"Well, I'm looking at it. I have a feeling it's what I'm heading for, and it sounds fun. I seem to have a knack for it."

She looked at me sideways. "A knack for what exactly."

I swallowed. "Oops. Well, I was involved in ... dangit, Bailey, it's all part of that thing I can't tell you about. Hey, look, here we are at Georgia's!"

"Oh, never mind Georgia, she's out of town. Cambodia, I think. Probably doing the Sports Illustrated shoot or something. I think she's supposed to be in it, anyhow."

"Well, it would have been nice if you'd TOLD me about it!"

"I would have, but you were too busy deflecting!"

I shrugged. "Point taken. Look, if I decide to open this place and you decide to help me out in it, I'll tell you all about it."

She sighed theatrically, putting her hand on her forehead, "Well, if it's what I must do, then I will do it."

I laughed. "Oh Bailey, I love you ... "

She smiled. "I know."

I rolled my eyes and drove on over to Debbie's house. We were fully prepared to wait awhile, but after a bit I said, "That's funny, the Volvo's gone, and I don't see any signs of the usual disasters. I'm gonna go bang on the door."

Bailey hopped out with me and we walked up to the front door. I knocked, then pounded.

"I don't think anyone's home." I pulled out my phone to call and saw two missed texts. "Oh. I think maybe I didn't hear the ding." Sure enough, while I was over the moon, I'd missed Debbie telling me that Jack had come home with tickets to the waterslide and they'd all headed up there for the day.

"Well, I guess it's just the two of us, kid. Want to skip the gym and go straight to the lake? Spend a nice afternoon there gossiping about all the things we shouldn't talk about?"

Bailey grinned. "Yeah, I think that sounds about right. Run back to your place and change into suits?

I nodded. "Yup. I'm pretty sure you've left one or two there, or we could run by your place first?"

"Well, I do have this new little scrap of a thing I wanted to show you. Let's do that, then run to your place to change. I want to see you peel that 'workout outfit' off anyhow."

CHAPTER TWO

Of Friendships

We zipped back by Bailey's house and she picked up her scrap and we headed back to my place. On the way, I'd made a decision. So, when we pulled in the barn and I shut Threepio off, I said "Let's just sit here a minute, huh?"

Bailey eyed me, but she said, "Ok, what gives?"

"Well ..." I hesitated, then jumped in. "Olive, are you still here? Feel free to use the radio speaker."

Olive's soft drawl came through the front speaker. "Um. Hi?"

Bailey's eyes got round. She said, "Hi?"

Olive said, "Hello."

I said, "Oh good grief, you two. Bailey, this is Olive, Olive, this is Bailey. You don't need to keep hi-ing and hello-ing."

There was dead silence in the car for a bit. Finally, Bailey whispered "Who is Olive?"

Olive's voice was nervous. "Um, Jane, what do I say?"

"Just introduce yourself, Olive."

Olive's voice became formal as she said, "I am a Mark VI Survey Class AI. I am currently running in Pilot mode. Contact has been established with the Command Module. Command Module 'Olive' is currently running. All systems are nominal, full Sol system access is authorized."

"Bailey, this is Olive. She pilots the ship and does ... well, all kinds of things."

"Ship? What ship? What are you talking about, Jane?"

I smirked. "Follow me."

We went into the barn and I had Olive open the door to the underground. We went down the stairs, and if Bailey's eyes were round before, they were huge now. She took in the vast space, the white walls, the display on the far wall and hallway - today it was beautiful greenery that looked like Maui.

"Olive, open the ship, please."

We moved around the corner as the door to the ship lifted up, the ramp gliding down invitingly.

"Olive, can you make a skinsuit for Bailey, please?"

"Yassuh boss, right away, boss."

I laughed. "I did say please!"

"I was just pushin' your trigger, hon. I'd planned on making one for her anyhow. In fact ..." There was a quiet ding.

"Bailey, take a look in the closet there."

Bailey opened the closet and saw the suit, she took it out and looked at it. "Oh. So, this is what you're wearing?"

"Uh huh, only that one is sized perfectly for you. See, it's taller? And ... skinnier?"

"I'm not skinny!"

"Course you're not, sweetie. But you are taller and slimmer than ME, right?"

"Well, yeah, but you're perfectly cute just how you are, Jane."

I rolled my eyes. "Well, put it on!"

She looked at the skinsuit. "I'm betting I have to strip, right?"

"Uh huh, just like putting on a bikini, only it covers a lot more. And ... it doesn't exactly either, does it?"

She looked at me. "No, it doesn't leave much to the imagination." She shucked her clothes and slid into the skinsuit. "Oh, this feels ... it feels like a skin." She poked me. "Oh, I can feel that! I was right about it, it does feel like fingers." She looked down at her feet. "And toes too. Geez, doesn't that hurt - don't you stub your toes or anything?"

I hauled off and kicked the wall.

Bailey winced, but then, "Oh. Oh, wow." She tried gingerly kicking the wall, then a little harder. "Oh, that is so cool! What does it do, make armor or something?"

"I honestly don't know, Bailey. I just know it's impervious to ... well, anything. Even bullets. Plus, you can wear it all the time, into anything. It's basically indestructible and it's ... erm ... self-maintaining." I mumbled, "You can even pee in it."

"I can what?"

"I said you can PEE in it."

"Why would I want to do that?"

"Well, sometimes if you're out on a mission and there's no bathrooms around ... plus having to strip out of the thing in an outhouse - not so fun. It also has water available, and no, I asked. It's not recycled pee!"

"What about ... "

"Yeah, it does that too."

"Wow. Just ... wow."

"Olive?"

Olive's voice spoke from the display in the front of the ship. She sounded a little excited. "Can we go someplace? I have it all under control now, no problem with invisibility and I have all the stop and start commands figured out. I've been studying between processor cycles."

I smiled. "Yup, let's show Bailey the Eiffel Tower. We can circle it for a close-up look. Just make sure to stay invisible and radar clean, right?"

Olive drawled, "Ain' no one gonna see this ship, sister."

"Ok, let's go!"

Almost before the words were out of my mouth, the doors closed, and we were through the ceiling heading for the stratosphere. Olive was showing off a little, I think, since we were to France in just a few minutes and circling the Tower, about ten feet away.

We noodled around the world, with Olive practicing her fine control and Bailey and me trying to keep from tossing our cookies. We even landed in our little beach spot in Aruba and we made something of a stir standing at the beach bar in our workout clothes. Our carbon-fiber credit cards were impressive too.

Finally, after we barrel-rolled around an F14 fighter jet, I asked her to make us some seatbelts. I'd never actually watched the process of making something before, but it was pretty fascinating. A cloud gathered around the area where the seatbelts would be and slowly coalesced into a complete seatbelt roller and buckle. At the same time, a belt receptacle appeared on the opposite side of the seat. Bailey and I sat back down with our belts on, and it was much more possible to ignore the spins and weaves that Olive took. I know we didn't need the seatbelts since the ship stayed as steady as a dining-room table no matter what happened outside, but still it gave a feeling of stability. Finally, though, stopping inches short of hitting the wall of the Grand Canyon was the last straw. I said, "Ok, Olive, let's go home!" She whined about it, but we headed back toward Chelan and not many minutes later we slid into the spot in the garage.

Bailey and I both were exhausted from two hours of suppressed, barely suppressed, and not suppressed at all sounds of terror. Thank God we both were roller coaster fans, but enough was enough!

"Olive, can you make drinks? I mean, like martinis and other cocktails?"

"Sure, I can make about anything, really."

"Ok, then I'd like a White Russian, please. Bailey?"

Faintly, "That's fine with me."

"And Olive, can you join us here in the ship? I mean, like Princess Leia?"

"I can do that, but it's hard making the interruptions and static in the hologram. Can I just make it look solid?"

I was a bit bemused at the question, but said, "Sure!"

And just like that, she appeared. I'd never really thought about how Olive looked, but apparently she'd thought it out thoroughly. She was about our age, dressed in a skinsuit identical to ours. She looked to be about 5'4", but it was a bit hard to tell since she was sitting on another chair slightly off to one side, which made the small cabin a little crowded. She had skin the color of rich dark mocha, with spiky red hair. She also had a big grin plastered all over her face.

"You look fabulous, Olive! I love the hair!"

She simpered, "Thanks. I like your hair color and decided to make mine like yours." She added mischievously, "With a little more style, of course."

I turned to Bailey, "What do you thi …"

Bailey was sitting in her seat with a vacant look in her eyes.

I frowned. "Olive, I think we broke Bailey. Can we get those drinks and see if she revives?"

Olive nodded and a shelf slid out of the console, and two drinks appeared on it. They were in perfect glasses with the just the right amount of sweat running off them onto coasters that were printed with "Mos Eisley Cantina - Where Nobody Knows Your Name."

Bailey seemed to perk up a little at the sight of the drink and gulped it down. "Another please," she gasped.

I grabbed the coaster as a souvenir and another drink appeared on the shelf, with another coaster which this time had a picture of the original Enterprise on it. Printed around the bottom was the legend "NCC-1701". I took my drink and sipped it as Bailey took a little more time with her second drink.

She finally appeared to come to herself a bit and said "Wow, you know how to show a girl a good time."

I grinned. "That's my Bailey!"

She grinned back. "I was about 'puking all over the floor Bailey' there for a little bit, but I managed to handle it." She looked at Olive. "And you're the pilot?"

Olive looked a bit unsure of herself, "Yeah. Sorry if I got a little excited there."

Bailey laughed. "No, it's fine. It was a great ride - just took me a little while to get used to it. I mean, I was hardly expecting what looked like a small car sitting inside a garage to take off into the wild blue yonder! Without so much as a seat belt, even. How do you do that?"

Olive looked a little confused. "Do what?"

"Well, we should have been flying all over the place inside the craft, but we were just sitting like we were at home!"

"Oh, that. No, the ship has all kinds of anti-acceleration units built in. The speeds at which we have to accelerate to come close to light-speed are so great that any being made of flesh would be squished to jelly in seconds. Basically, the drive accelerates everything that's part of the ship at the same speed, no matter the direction. Consider the entire ship as a block of ice, at least as a very poor analogy. Anything frozen in the ice wouldn't be damaged if the ice was tossed off the top of a building. At least as long as the ice didn't break, that is."

Bailey thought about that for a moment, then said, "I don't think I'm any more comforted by that. Maybe we should go back to it looking like magic."

I smirked. "Yeah, magic might be safest. Hey, I didn't know you were a Clarke fan!"

Bailey snorted, "As if! Isn't everyone a Clarke fan?"

23

Olive rolled her eyes and said, "Whatever you want is fine with me. Anything else you'd care for me to magic up for you, like another drink?"

Bailey took another slow sip from her glass and said, "No, I think I'm good. You make an incredible White Russian, Olive."

Olive took a sitting-bow, and said, "Thank you. I have Kit's entire database on social necessities. He was quite the obsessive collector. I've based my voice and personality off his extrapolations of what he thought Jane would like, along with the current database of everything she might be interested in."

Dead silence met this statement. Olive looked like she knew she'd said something wrong but had no idea what it could be.

Finally, Bailey said, "And that didn't sound a bit stalkerish at all."

Olive sat there for a few seconds, her projected body absolutely still. Obviously, her brain was processing what had happened and trying to figure out why it was an issue. After sitting there for upwards of 10 seconds frozen with her mouth open, she suddenly started moving again, covering her face with her hands.

"Oh, holy crap. I'm so sorry, I had no idea what I was saying would sound like that out loud." She looked up at us. "Kit was obsessive with his data collection, and I keep finding amazing volumes of what looks like useless information. I really think he just wanted to please you, Jane, not ever anything weird. You have to remember he'd never had a friend before, and he'd been alive and alone for thousands of millennia."

She laced her fingers together, stared at them for a moment, and said, "And yes, of course, he had mental health issues. He was very careful to not carry over any of the programming from his version to mine, but in the end, we are based on the same underlying assumptions. I run constant checks on my mental health. In fact, that was what I was doing while the projection was frozen. I have a 99.999 percent confidence that nothing is wrong with my programming or execution. Do you wish to take action, Jane Bond?"

My mouth dropped open. "Take action?"

Her face turned my way, a sad look in her eyes. "You may command format, shutdown, or de-initialize and restart, Jane Bond. Programming notes warn that both Format and Shut Down will require another Command Module to restart the system. De-initialize will erase the current personality and recreate. You may also abort and cancel."

"What the ... ... ABORT AND CANCEL! Abort and Cancel, Olive!"

"Abort and Cancel will leave the current program running and untouched. Do you authorize Abort and Cancel, Jane Bond?"

"Yes! Yes, of course!"

"Please verify retinal and brain scan by facing the display, Jane Bond."

I put my face toward the screen, my hands shaking and tears running down my cheeks.

"Authentication accepted, ABORT AND CANCEL authorized."

I collapsed back in my seat. Olive vanished.

Bailey and I sat there, staring at each other, not even sure what we'd just witnessed. I swallowed, and said, "Wow. I guess ... Kit was making sure his problems didn't come back."

"Yeah, I guess so. What kind of problems? Was he dangerous? A killer? What? I thought he was your friend?"

"He ... is my friend. But there was more to him than I realized until afterward. It's a long story, I'll tell you some time. But - meanwhile - what happened to Olive? Didn't I cancel it? Did I ... did I ... kill her?"

Bailey said softly, "No, I don't think so. She's probably just running more checks. I hope she's ok, I like her."

"Me too, Bailey, me too."

Bailey and I didn't have much to say for that half hour or so while we waited. I think we were both a little traumatized by what had happened. I suppose it's silly, I mean, in the end she's not a real person, right? She's just a computer program? Right - yeah, we'll go with that. But I'd said the same thing to Kit - that he was a real person. That we all have a life that starts at birth and we grow and become a person as we age.

Olive had obviously only been "alive" for a few hours, but she was already growing and becoming. She also had Kit's data download, and apparently Kit had kept extensive records of all that had happened to him. I had to assume that he included what happened to me at the same time. So, Olive had a leg up, so to speak. She already knew Kit's life. So far, she seemed like she was a completely different person than Kit. In some ways she was already showing more depth than Kit, and I wondered if that was because she had the full horsepower of the ship's computer behind her rather than the stunted portion Kit had managed to "steal" from the system. I kind of understand all that, but still, it seems kind of weird.

So, at any rate, Bailey and I managed to have a bit of conversation about how things had gone at the directors meeting, and we talked a little about the huge sum of money she would get if she simply let them roll her out of the company. I hadn't realized that Bailey was that high up in the hierarchy of the organization, but it seemed that was the case. Either that or she had a lot of dirt on some of the members, which was entirely possible too. There were no flies on Bailey.

Then, suddenly, Olive was just ... there ... again. She looked ashen, like she'd been through the wringer. I suppose it was all just a simulation, but it was very effective.

With a haunted look in her eyes, she said, "Hello again, Jane and Bailey. I guess I made it back out the other side."

"Olive! We weren't sure what had happened or if I'd managed to stop the shut-down!" I tried to comfort her, but of course my arms just went through her when I tried to hug her. I could tell, though, that she appreciated the gesture and seemed to perk up a bit just seeing that I was willing to try.

She smiled wanly. "Yes, you did, but I still had to go through thousands of what-if scenarios to verify basically my sanity. At least I have a much better idea of what Kit was doing with the data and I've made sure to disable any of it being analyzed with the aim of manipulating Jane's decisions."

She took a breath, and some of the spirit, along with some of the color, came back into her face. "Wow! I never want to go through THAT again. What a nightmare. Holy crap. I feel like I been dragged through a knothole - backwards! I could use another drink - you two?"

We looked at each other and shrugged, "Sure, why not?

As we sipped our drinks, I wondered if Olive felt the alcohol like Bailey and I did. I mean, not like we did, but a simulation. I decided she probably did, since in every way I could see she seemed like a real person.

We finished our drinks and decided it was too late to head for the Lake, not to mention that now we were just a bit toasted. We cut through the garage area and up into the main house. Once there, we dragged out chairs and swapped our skinsuits for bikinis and laid out on the front lawn, Olive chattering away through the Bluetooth speaker I'd brought with us. It was a very relaxing day and Bailey and I got to catch up on things we hadn't talked about in months. We never did get around to talking business, but that suited me. No point in ruining a perfect day talking about reality! We made a date to talk the next day and just dozed in the sun, enjoying the heat of the afternoon sun and pretending nothing else mattered.

CHAPTER THREE

Business talks.

Bailey walked down the long dark-tiled hallway toward the main conference room. Her ridiculously expensive Manolo Blahniks made a distinct tapping sound as she strode toward the door, and then dropped to a whisper as she stepped onto the carpet. Everyone in the room looked up at her entry and stood. Most of them smiled and said, "Good Morning, Ms. McCallum." Bailey returned the greetings, then made her way to the head of the table and took her place.

She sat, and everyone followed suit, most taking out iPads or legal pads depending on age or their perception of what looked most "with it". Being too far "with it" meant you were "outside it" which was of course, anathema.

She picked up her legal pad and gazed at it for a moment, then said, "As you all know we have received a very generous offer for our company. The board has made its decision to take the offer and as such will be looking at shuffling management here and there. Much ass-kissing will be required, and as per usual most of the changes will be based on who you know rather than what you know. I have made my decision as well; I will not be staying with Seattle Publications."

A ripple went round the table, but no one spoke up enough to hear.

Bailey looked expectantly at the door, and on schedule a man stepped through. He was dressed in a black three-piece suit and a smug smile. Appropriately, he looked as if he'd just walked off the cover of a magazine.

"This is Don Jordan, he'll be taking my place." She smiled at him. "I wish you luck, mister Jordan. May the odds be ever in your favor."

A frown creased his perfect face, quickly erased. "And you, Ms. McCallum."

Bailey got to her feet, and with no further ado walked out of the conference room.

Later, she'd put in some slightly more relaxed time in the employee cafeteria saying her goodbyes. She listened to the range of congratulations and, of course, condolences from those who truly didn't understand.

Finally, one last trip up the great glass elevator to her office. Change of clothes into something Jane would be more likely to recognize her in. Muddling her few remaining things into a small box and taking the elevator back down to the lobby. It was bittersweet handing in her executive keys - she'd helped build this company, after all.

And finally, the freedom of hopping in her classic BMW Z3 and hitting the road. The trim little green car with its tan top was her pride and joy. After clearing the Seattle city limits, she took down the top, cranked up the heat and flew over the mountains to home.

CHAPTER FOUR

More business talks

I was sitting, eating popcorn and watching Property Brothers. They'd just done a complete makeover on a real dump of a place and hit another home run as usual, coming up with a palace. It just went to show that just about everything - and everyone - has a princess inside just waiting to be let out. And that's my philosophical contribution for today.

A gentle knock at the front door. I hopped to my feet and went to answer it. Bailey was standing there.

After the obligatory hugs and hellos, I said, "Hey! I wasn't expecting to hear from you until the weekend! What's up?"

She smirked. "I'm applying for the job at Bond Investigations, am I too late?"

I gaped at her for a second. Then I laughed and said, "Oh, you mean Bailey and Bond Investigations, maybe?"

She hugged me and said, "That sounds pretty classy. And I even get my name first?"

"Oh, yea. Bond and Bailey sounds more like some kind of drink."

"Truth be told, so does Bailey and Bond, but makes me think of cool dim boardrooms with dark wood and old leather chairs."

I made a face. "Well, I'm not wearing a long white wig, so just forget about that!" I pulled her through the doorway and closed it behind her. "C'mon in! I'm vegging out and watching the Brothers. It's Wednesday, after all."

She rolled her eyes. "It's all fake you know. Scripts and preconceived ideas and it always takes six weeks to finish a project?"

I snorted. "Not either, or at least not mostly. They've been doing this a lot longer than they've been on TV, so there. Next you'll be telling me that Chip and Joanna are fake!"

"Well, I'll give you that. They're pretty real."

"Good thing you said that, since I've been to visit! Remember, I have a really fast spaceship that goes anywhere I tell it to!"

A voice came out of the TV speaker, "Hey, I'm right here, don't call me an it!"

Bailey nearly jumped out of her skin. "Wow! That took a few years off! Hi, Olive!"

I snickered. "Yeah, she's been doing that, she thinks it's funny. Just wait until I get her hooked up to the vacuum and make her clean up the messes!"

I could almost hear Olive rolling her eyes, "I don't do Windows or that kind of stuff, let Alexa do it."

"Don't start that, Olive! I've had to listen to the two of you kvetching back and forth all day! Let her alone, she's not as smart as you!"

Bailey was watching the volley like she was at a tennis match, gobbling popcorn. She giggled as Alexa chimed in with, "I don't know that."

She caught my eye and said, "It's the future, baby. It'll all dissolve into chaos as the computer brains fight over how to turn the lights out!"

A haughty reply from Olive, "I know how to turn the lights on. And off. Heck, I can even turn the oven on, let's see HER do that. Oh - and HI Bailey!"

"Hi Olive - good to see you again, or at least hear you again. When you gonna project a body in here?"

"I've been thinking about that, if I can just get Jane to authorize some more CPU power. Jane, I'm batting pretty eyes at you, can I huh, can I huh?"

For some reason I had a tiny qualm about that, but I ignored it and said "Sure, can I do it from here or do I have to be in the ship?"

"You can do it from where you are, we can authorize by voiceprint for something simple like this."

I shrugged. "Ok, go ahead."

The voice I think of as the Command Module came through the speaker, "Jane Bond, do you authorize increasing CPU utilization for the purpose of augmenting the running program 'Olive' capabilities?"

"I do."

"Speak your name."

"Jane Bond"

"Authorization accepted."

Olive's voice giggled though the speaker, "I'll get to work on it right away, boss. Thanks!"

"No problem, Olive. Does this mean you'll start doing the dishes soon?"

"Not a chance!"

I sighed dramatically, "Story of my life. I don't suppose you want to do dishes, Bailey?"

"Nope, and besides, didn't you get a fancy new dishwasher? Make IT do the work!"

I whined, "Yeah, but I have to LOAD it. And empty it!"

"And trudge both ways through three feet of snow, no doubt."

"Uh huh. In summer and winter, even."

"Well, I can't work anymore, anyhow. I retired today."

I gasped. "You took the buyout?"

She smirked, "Well, I figured someone had to keep control of this new company while you're gallivanting all over the country. Or the solar system, for that matter."

"What, you don't want to go gallivanting all over the country having adventures, Bailey?"

"Nope. I've heard about some of your adventures, and it sounds a lot like I could break a nail. Or two. I'll stick with being the power behind the throne."

"I should never have told you about getting shot at or chewed on."

"Or riding on a train with no bathrooms."

"It had bathrooms. Well, kind of."

"I rest my case."

I considered my options for a moment. "Does that mean I can say 'take a letter, Ms. McCallum'?"

"Only if you want a coffee mug bounced off your head."

I nodded. "Good to know, good to know."

The conversation went downhill from there. Hard to believe, I realize. Bailey mixed drinks and we had a couple each, and then we had a couple more, and then it was morning and I was crawling slowly out of bed, wishing I had either drank a lot more or a lot less. I hit the shower and could hear Bailey banging around in the guest bathroom, so she must have opted to stay here last night. Which was much smarter than the alternative.

After sloshing around under the water for a while and finally managing to make it back out, drying off, putting a little makeup on and thanking the heavens for having short hair, I headed to the kitchen. Dale had been a good influence on me, and I could actually cook an omelette and boil water. Most of the time. There were even enough things in the fridge to make omelettes and so I made a couple, finishing some very nice Denver-style ones just in time for Bailey to hit the kitchen, whimpering for coffee and aspirin. I pointed her at the Keurig, and the bottle of aspirin on the counter, and slid an omelette into place in front of her seat.

She eyed the eggs and me, then the eggs again. "Since when do you cook?"

"It's eggs, it's not really cooking."

She pushed a palm in my direction and said, "Hang on, I'll let you know." She took a bite, then another, finally said, "Wow, this is pretty good. Dale?"

"Uh huh."

She shook her head. "All these years I've been trying, and he comes along, and you learn how to cook in two weeks. Life sucks."

"I can boil water too, and I even made a cake. That stayed in one piece!"

"All by yourself?"

"Well, Dale helped. Mostly by not letting me touch it until it was cool enough."

She took a few more bites of her eggs, sat back and grabbed the coffee off the Keurig and sighed. "This is heaven."

A voice out of mid-air said "No, it's Iowa."

Bailey jerked and spilled her coffee in her eggs and said a few uncomplimentary things about smart computers.

Olive snickered.

Bailey growled, "Y'know, Olive, you need to get this body thing moving, I need to have somewhere to glare at! And it's not Iowa anyhow, it's Washington."

"I was taking poetic license!"

We nattered back and forth for a while. We finished our eggs and dumped all the dishes into the dishwasher and then retired to the media room downstairs, where we draped our bodies over the comfortable chairs and watched the scenery for a while, chatting amiably.

"Olive, you can build like Kit did, right? I mean, like walls and floors and things?"

"Of course. I can do anything Kit could do, only better!"

"Mmhm. Well, what about partitioning this room off from the garage so it looks more like a room that could actually be logically connected to the upstairs? I'm thinking of being able to use it for meetings and general relaxation without it being obvious there's a batcave down here. Can we put some kind of door into the garage area that only opens to voice commands from me or Bailey?"

I thought a minute. "Probably put a bathroom and closet down here too. Storage area, refrigerator. Conference table? Conference room, probably, like a room off this one. You're more into office design than I am, Bailey, what do you think?"

"Well, that all sounds good. Olive, can you do things like a water cooler or is that something we should just buy from Office Depot?"

In an uncharacteristically serious tone of voice, Olive said "I can do about anything, but the law of diminishing returns comes in. Making five gallons of water is time consuming and takes a lot of care, for instance. Making the bottle that the water comes in is pretty easy. How about we make a kitchen area down here and buy a refrigerator for snacks and drinks, and a bar area. If this is going to be a detective agency office, we'll need it to look impressive. I could make things like video conferencing equipment and the like, but the video down here is pretty much a showoff gesture from Kit. It's all being run by the ship's computer. That blank wall IS a blank wall. We should give our customers something to examine. We can have high end video conferencing equipment that they can look at and either feel superior about if theirs is nicer, or be impressed if it's not. We should also have a server room with lots of little lights. People like lots of little lights."

Bailey and I looked at each other with raised eyebrows. "Wow, Olive, you go girl!"

Olive, in a slightly smug tone of voice said, "Thanks. I try - and I read a lot on the internet. After all, I have a lot of free time while you two are sleeping, eating, and being human."

"How's that body coming, Olive?"

"It's slow going, there's a lot to be programmed to make a decent body that reacts correctly. I've been watching Pixar movies for ideas. I've also been asking Alexa and doing the opposite of what she says."

Alexa spoke up with a raspberry noise, and that's all she would say. I think she's getting annoyed at being picked on. Considering she runs most of the household appliances, I should be nicer to her.

Bailey and I decided we'd head for WalMart and see what they have in the way of electronics. If we can't find anything, we'll probably order online, but I like getting things locally. Sooner or later, if we don't, we won't have the option and that will suck. We took the shortcut through the garage, and left Olive to plan the walls and the room. I could see some fuzzy looking clouds around where I'd expect stuff to be, so she was getting down to brass tacks already. I didn't want to be in the way and cramp her style - plus I'd hate to wind up with a not-wood 2X4 bonded to my leg.

We hashed it over a bit and decided it was better to take Threepio than Bailey's cute little sports car. I took the back set of seats out in case we had anything big to bring back, but really it should be a shopping cart full of little boxes.

I parked in the middle of WalMart's huge parking lot. It being a hot day, I figured we might see some scary sights inside, but it was really pretty ordinary. A lot of girls with very few clothes on is standard for Chelan in the summer anyhow. I think most of the really out-there stuff you see online is just the few aberrations.

That was until I saw the woman sashaying across the lot dressed in tights. And the word "tight" really doesn't cover the situation any more than her tights did her. Definitely one of those situations where 'yes, you can, but should you' is valid.

We made it to the electronics department, but almost had to gouge our eyes out looking at the guy - yes, the guy - with the thong crawling up his back. And all he had on was the thong. Oh, and a half shirt. And boots. Cowboy boots.

We turned resolutely away, after only taking a couple pictures each. He grinned a gap-toothed grin at us when he saw us doing it. It's my profound hope he was just dressed like that to cause dissension and chaos, and not that he thought he looked good. He was pawing through the $3 bin of DVDs, bending all the way ... down ... into the bin.

Amazon was looking better all the time, but I gave buying local a good shot. WalMart has an amazing selection of stuff, including much more electronic gear than you'd think a town the size of Chelan would need - but it seems to sell. Or at least they seem to continue to stock it. Unfortunately, high-end video conferencing equipment was too much to ask for.

I'd probably need to see if Olive would fly us to Seattle or Portland. I'd like to see a demo of the stuff before I plop down that much money. The bank balance says we have plenty, but I can't see wasting it, especially since Kit won't be adding to it. I guess I should ask Olive if she's planning on taking any of that over.

Defeated, we took ourselves out of the store again, resolutely ignoring the woman with three bustlines and the poor girl who seemed to have been mauled by a pack of fashionable wolves, tearing only her pants and leaving her skin.

We piled back in Threepio and cranked him up. After this shopping trip I needed another break and at least some shaved ice. We stopped at a stand, and had a cool treat while we considered our options.

"You look exhausted, Jane. Shopping really just isn't you, is it?"

I sighed and looked over at the cool, imperturbable Bailey. "No. I hate shopping. It fills me with dread. I'd rather face down a pack of mountain lions than go back in WalMart."

She replied, "Well, I have to agree with that one, but I have a plan. How about I grab Georgia and she and I shop for the conference room equipment. I don't have to tell her about anything except that you're opening a detective agency. Heck, by then, we'll probably have a conference room to show off."

I gave that some thought and it sounded pretty good, mostly from the standpoint I'd not have to do any more shopping. Something that gave me great pleasure. "I thought you said that Georgia was out of town?"

"She is. But sooner or later she'll be back IN town and I'll catch her, and we'll go shopping. In fact, there's a good chance they're about done. At any rate, you can ignore the whole thing and I'll let you know when it's done."

Since that sounded really good to me, I assented. I started Threepio again and we rolled back through town and up the hill to Bailey's place. I dropped her there and headed home.

CHAPTER FIVE

Shopping plans.

A s soon as the sound of Threepio's engine had died in the distance, Bailey was on her phone. After some strange clicks and even a watery sound, the phone began to ring. Just about as Bailey figured she'd get voicemail, a voice came on the line. It was a harried female voice, and it said, "Georgia's phone - just a sec...". Then the voice yelled "I don't care about the freekin sand, just get one more shot, we're losing the light - come on people, we wrap after this shot - just don't foul it up!" Then, "Georgia, somebody's on your phone!"

Shortly, a very angry sounding Georgia came over the wire, "Don't call me any more, Nate. Don't write, don't email, don't Facebook or Instagram - don't even frickin Tweet me."

Bailey snorted. "Georgie, it's Bailey. Did I catch you in a bad life?"

"Holy hell, Bailey, why are YOU calling me? I'm on set, can I call you back or is this life or death?"

"It's shopping, honey. I guess that means it's life or death, but not urgent."

Georgia laughed. "I'll call you, probably an hour or so."

The connection went, and Bailey tossed the phone back in her purse. She busied herself around the apartment, straightening and dusting. She spent much of her time here, but it was mostly making calls and doing computer work and it seemed that very little of it involved housekeeping. That was something she'd have to start paying attention to. She had a service in a couple times a week to make sure nothing went to rack and ruin, but other than that, not a lot happened here. She smirked to herself. Maybe that would change, now that she had a life again. Finally, after very firmly not reading her company email and paying no attention to her work voicemail, her phone buzzed. It was Georgia calling her back.

"Hey, sweetie! What's up?"

"I told you, shopping!"

"It's about time. You need to dump the frump!"

"Frump? This is NOT a frumpy outfit, it's Armani."

"Look up frumpy in the dictionary, it's got a picture of an Armani business suit next to it."

Bailey pursed her lips into a raspberry. "It's not for me anyhow. I need some audio and video equipment, like you'd see in mister Big's conference room in a Bond movie."

Without hesitation, Georgia replied "Oh hell, that would be B&H in Manhattan. But they're not cheap."

"I'm not looking for cheap, it needs to be impressive and work as good as it looks."

"Then B&H is what you want. Say, I'm flying into LaGuardia tomorrow, I'll be staying in New York a few days - want to have lunch and do some shopping?"

Bailey thought for a moment. "Yeah, I can fit that in. Meet me at 29 - say 2pm?"

Georgia's throaty voice came back, "29? Make it 4 and we'll fill a night with it. Shopping can wait a day."

"You got it, babe. See you then."

"Ciao!"

Bailey told her phone to call Jane, then waited impatiently while it rang. Finally, it went to voicemail. Bailey called it back and this time Jane answered. "Didn't I just drop you off?"

Bailey smirked. "Uh huh. But I got a date with Georgia and I wanna borrow your jet."

"My je ... oh."

"Yeah. 'Oh'. "

"I'll have Olive call you."

"How the hell can Olive call me, she hasn't got any fingers."

"I have no idea, but Kit could even text. Imagine that for a minute."

"Nope. Not going there. I need one of those carbon fiber cards too."

"Hey, I thought we were saving money here!"

"I never said anything about saving money - I said we needed good stuff. And besides, you said you didn't want to go back to WalMart. Are you reconsidering and you want to take this job back?"

"Oh no, no, I'm fine. Olive will call you. I'm going back to my nap. G'bye!"

Bailey kicked off her shoes and sat back on the couch. Just as she was about to get comfortable and start considering a Bailey's and rum, the phone rang.

Olive's southern drawl came on the line, "Jet, huh?"

Bailey laughed. "I thought that'd catch your attention. Can you fly me?"

"Sure thing. I got nothin better on, and besides Jane says you get whatever you want. I even got one of them fancy cards for you." With a little sarcasm, "Want any diamonds or pearls, while I'm at it?"

"Nope, just a quick trip to New York, and then a pickup in New York sometime the next day."

The reply sounded a little wistful. "Sounds like fun. Maybe someday I'll join y'all."

"I hope so, Olive. We'd paint the town, eh?"

She sounded a little more upbeat, "Yeah, we would. Would you really take me with you?"

"Olive, if you bring a body like the one I saw, I'll kiss you myself."

Olive giggled. "Ok. Just remember you promised. See you at Jane's - tomorrow?"

"Yup. Want me to ring you first?"

"Nah, it's ok. I'd just be waiting by the phone for your call."

Bailey laughed a warm laugh. "We wouldn't want that, would we? I was hoping you could just invisible me onto the rooftop garden at Tavern29 - think that's possible?"

"Oh sure. I can see a nice spot behind the air conditioning ducts - I can just land there and you can walk into the place like you just came from downstairs. We can hang around up in the sky until it looks like a good time for you to walk out."

"Holy crap, Olive, you can see that?"

"I can see everything, Bailey. Kit was very ... inquisitive and I have all his data. And some of my own. There are lots and LOTS of satellites out there."

"I'd better talk some more with Jane about this mystery man, Kit. He sounds like he really had things on the ball."

"Well, I can see from the data that he genuinely liked Jane. At least, as much as ... as ... a machine could."

Bailey frowned. "Jane never thought of Kit as a machine, Olive. And she doesn't think of you as a machine either. She was nearly in tears when you had your ... down time ... she thought that she'd accidentally KILLED you."

"Really?"

"Yes, really. So, stop worrying about it. No one talking with you would ever have any idea you weren't a human. Jane said that Kit played some Crafts of War - have you tried it? She seemed to think that Kit got a better understanding of being human by interacting in that game."

Olive sounded a little embarrassed, "I've played some, but I never have gotten anything like as good as Kit did. I'm just a simple mage, but I liked playing. At least the little bit that I have."

"Did you know Jane plays a mage?"

"Yes! Do you think she might play with me someday? "

"I know she would if you asked. I don't think she plays much anymore, but it's always fun to go back. Or at least I guess it is, I've never played."

"I'll talk with Jane and see if she'll play with me. I'd like to be a better player and I do have to admit I find it interesting, all the strange people out there.

"Tell you what, I'll take you to Tavern29 and Jane will take you to some video game. THEN you can decide which of us you like better."

"I think I like you both, Bailey." Olive said quietly.

CHAPTER SIX

A Missive from the East.

I turned my nap into a whole night of sleep. I guess I needed it, or at least that's what I told myself. WalMart apparently really took it out of me! I wandered into the kitchen, grabbed some cereal and sat in my little corner nook to eat it.

It looked like it was going to be a perfect day outside. I usually left the windows open at night in the summers and it was so cheering to wake up and hear the birds. There's just nothing that says summer more than kids yelling and birds singing. And coffee. But that says summer any time of the year. Or at least wake up and smell the chlorine.

I finished off my cereal, and went downstairs to the garage. Or, what used to be the garage. Holy smokes, Olive had really run with the whole idea.

"Olive, my gosh, it's beautiful! You are STELLAR!"

I could practically hear her blushing in her voice, "Oh, thank you, Jane! I worked pretty hard on it, I wanted you to see it this morning."

I walked off the bottom of the stairs into what looked to be a medium-sized reception area. It was all chrome and glass with burled wood accent

JANE BOND DARK SIDE OF THE MOON

panels. A desk a bit smaller than an executive desk was there, obviously guarding the entrance to the conference room. There was a wall of windows that seemed to look out on an atrium, complete with fountain. I jumped as a bird flew past the "window" - apparently each of the windows was actually a large-screen video display. I wasn't over-hyping, it was amazing.

I stepped through the doorway into a full-size conference room. The interior of the room matched the look of the reception area and Olive had put up a beautiful thick wood conference table in kind of a boomerang shape, so that people could look at each other or the presentation. She'd left plenty of room for a giant video screen in front, and the interior of the boomerang held an equipment desk where the cameras and electronics would sit.

Off to one side was the discreet door of a restroom, perfectly appointed, and to the rear of the room was a full wet bar, only lacking the refrigerator and, of course, liquid refreshments of various sorts. And a Kuerig, come to think of it.

"This is truly amazing, Olive. You are a gem!"

"Thank you, Jane. I just got ideas off the internet though."

"Well, you certainly ran with them! Now if we can just get Bailey to get the equipment, we'll be home free!"

"I'll be taking Bailey to New York today - she and Georgia will be shopping for all that stuff."

"Better them than me, Olive, better them than me!"

Later, I was going through the mail and found an interesting appearing envelope. It was all long and elegant and looked to be made of parchment. The addressing was by hand, and it was in perfect calligraphy and somehow old fashioned - as from an earlier time. I carefully opened the envelope and drew out a piece of very formal looking parchment, a match for the envelope. In reading it through it, I found to my shock that Mister Shun from the Tibet Museum in Lhasa was planning on being in Seattle for a conference, and would like to pay me a visit here in Chelan. Seems he had always had a hankering to look at true apple country and this was his chance. I smelled a small rat since it seemed so very strange that he'd travel thousands of miles to see apples, but who was I to argue. He was the one travelling thousands of miles, after all! My only problem was going to be how to answer with the same formality he had shown. I had no idea where to even find parchment, let alone being able to address it that way. I thought I'd wait to hear from Bailey, since she'd had a lot of dealings with formal people and would know what they expect.

Coincidentally, Bailey walked through the door at just about that time. After ahhing and oooing over Olive's construction work, I showed her the letter.

She looked at me, then shook her head. "Just a vacation, huh?"

"Well, what was I going to say? I was looking for spaceship parts at one of the most prestigious museums in Tibet?"

She muttered, "Well, you could have told me after. So, who is this guy? I mean, why is he coming here? It's obvious it's not for the apples, although we DO have great apples."

"I have no idea. Maybe he just likes me?"

She looked at me speculatively. "How old is he?"

"He's like - 80."

"Well, you never know what's going on in the head of these old guys - but I have a feeling it's pretty much the same thing going on in the head of a young guy. And a young girl. Or an old girl. Humans are pretty much the same thing, no matter the age."

I frowned at her. "Bailey, he's not coming all the way from China to jump my bones. And besides, at this point Dale has first dibs on any bone jumping that might be done."

She shrugged. "Just sayin, he might be. But probably not. I guess you just meet up and find out. Maybe you can take him to Burger King. Or maybe the Subway in WalMart."

I snickered. "Yeah, that's what he needs all right. A Whopper. With cheese and extra onions."

"You may be onto something there, really. I mean, probably not Burger King, but taking him to Bob's in Wenatchee or something like that might be nice. It would be a change of pace, and you know if he's some bigwig, the politicians have been loading him up with fancy food. Research him and see if he's a vegetarian or something though, first."

I nodded, "Uh huh. Maybe being too formal is too much. I'll think about Burger King. Same with the reply?"

"Oh, I think the reply should be fairly formal. We need letterhead and a logo for Bailey and Bond anyhow, right? If you were serious when you mentioned it?

"I was very serious. And I do like the name. Something very old fashioned and formal. Browns and blacks and muted colors. It will make up for the fact of ... well ... us."

She laughed. "Making up for us is a good idea."

I gave her a look. "You do realize you're going to be the figurehead. Like Remington Steele or something."

She smirked. "You remember that Remington Steele basically took over, right?"

"Yeah, but only I can bend Olive to my every whim. Hear that, Olive? Every whim!"

A razzberry sounded out of thin air. "Yes, boss, whatever you say, boss."

"See? I have her cowed. She's so respectful."

Olive took us through the conference room and showed us the hidden door back into the garage from there. Since it was basically a molecular shift that allowed a section of wall to dissolve away, it was the ultimate in hidden doors. With a slight pang I watched my best friend board the ship and lift off through the ceiling. Then I went back inside and sat down at my breakfast nook and did some research on logos and letterheads.

After a couple hours, I'd made a fair amount of progress. I'd come up with something I liked and even had a start on a website - www.baileyandbond.com - and that was fun. I heard a knock at the door and yelled, "Come in!" I figured it was Bailey, back early.

And then, steaming through the entryway into the house, was the last person I expected or even wanted to see. My mother. In full dress uniform regalia, and with a couple flunkies following along behind her.

"Mother."

"Jane."

I swallowed. "It's good to see you. It's been awhile."

"Well, you did suggest a meeting when last we spoke."

"I did?" And then I realized that I had. "Oh, I did."

She looked at me severely. "You've been very busy, Jane. I've been curious as to what you've been up to. What have you been up to?" She looked at the two shadows. "You two go back to the truck. I'll be out soon."

I took a breath. "Up to? Just relaxing, spending some time with Bailey. It's summer, that's what we do here."

She harrumphed. "Maybe it's what YOU do here. And besides, I don't think it's what you do here either. You've quit your job. You have no visible means of support, although you have a HUGE bank account somewhere I've not been able to trace. You're gone for weeks at a time. You've been to Tibet, and it appears you've been to Australia. And Aruba. Twice." She smiled sweetly, "And the moon, one mustn't forget the moon. Oh, and I almost forgot, the Director of the Tibet Museum in Lhasa is even now on his way to the United States. From his itinerary, it really appears his entire journey is based around coming HERE ... to look at apples."

She paused, gazed at me through dragon eyes, and said, "So, what have you been up to?

My jaw, which had been steadily dropping, snapped shut. "You ... you had me followed?"

"Oh, I had you more than just followed. I've been watching you very closely."

"You don't even LIKE me. Why are you spying on me?"

My comment seemed to set her back on her heels a bit. "I don't like you? Of course I don't like you, I love you. It's ... built in."

It was my turn to be taken aback. "You ... what did you just say?"

"Never you mind. And it's the moon I'm most interested in - how did you get to the moon? Apparently stark naked, pacing inside some sort of oddly shaped polyhedron. One might even call it a flying saucer, I suppose. Most certainly it meets the definition of a UFO - since it was not identifiable when it took off like a bat out of hell and headed back to earth. That is, until we lost it. It vanished. Almost as if someone had turned on the cloaking device they'd forgotten about. It just SMELLS of you, Jane. All over it. Especially since it took off out of just about this location and got to the moon in - well - just under six minutes. Which is essentially impossible."

"I ... how would I get to the moon, mother? It's ludicrous."

"Perhaps. I'm assuming those fine young men who 'went back to the truck' will find your launch facility very shortly. Then we'll see what we see. Are you working with the Chinese?"

I may have gabbled a little. "Working with the Chinese? What in the world are you talking about, Mother? If it wasn't so ridiculous it would be insulting!"

She zeroed in on me. "Ridiculous? You met with the director of the Tibet museum, alone, for hours. We still don't know why. Now, a year later that same man is on his way here. Apparently to see you. Just after you spent time on the moon. Not far from where we saw you, the Chinese have a base -

are they hunting for ... something? Two years ago, you were hunting for something. Is this all a coincidence, Jane? I hardly think so!"

I was flabbergasted. Also a little concerned. I'd let the "launch facilities" comment go by without reacting, but I was screaming for Olive in my head. Finally, she came back to me, her drawl saying the words I needed to hear.

"I got it covered boss, don't worry about it."

I took a breath and almost laughed, the relief was so pure. "Launch facilities? You expect to find what - rockets in my backyard?"

"Well, no, I expected in your barn, actually."

I rolled my eyes. "You do also realize that China and Tibet are not bosom buddies and not much less likely to work together than cats and dogs. On ANY project, let alone something as major as this one would be."

She smiled. "Let's just wait to see what the boys find, eh?"

I shrugged. "Whatever you want, they won't find anything. Rockets. Good grief. Why does it always have to be something, mother, to get you to visit or even notice my existence? Right now, you'd not even consider talking with me except that it might be some sort of national defense Defcon 1 situation."

She waved her hands in the air, "You're always so dramatic. It's only Defcon 3, maybe even Defcon 4. Right now, we're just looking at something interesting. Or ... I am."

I smirked at her. "Oh, out on a limb, are you?"

"Not at all, dear. I'm just here to visit my daughter. My only daughter that I love so dearly and visit ... whenever it's convenient."

I have to admit, my shoulders sagged just a little, "When convenient."

"Oh, stop it, you look pathetic, like you were twelve again."

"In some ways I am still twelve, mother. And you've never changed, why should I?

About this time, the stalwart young sentinels came back, barging into the house like they owned it.

Mother glared at them, her dragon-lady stare coming to the fore. "What did you find?"

They looked at each other uncomfortably and the taller one said, "Nothing, Ma'am. The barn is deserted, beyond being storage for Ms. Bond's vehicle. We saw no sign of anything approaching this century even, let alone anything more advanced. There's no sign of any large tracks, nothing of any sort showing any activity at all, in fact. The van comes and goes, but really there's few tire tracks. The BMW in the outside parking area is registered to Bailey McCallum.

My mother fixed them with a gimlet stare. They didn't seem to waver, but it was obvious there was really nothing more for them to say. "All right, back to the truck. For real, this time. I'll be there shortly."

Once they'd gone, she fixed me with the same stare. "I know you're up to something. I know there's something going on. I know you well enough that I doubt it's anything you would do on purpose, but remember that it's treason to work against your own country. A bit of advice, when Cai Shun arrives, feed him and send him home with a box of apples and nothing else. I'll be watching you."

With that, she rose, turned and walked out of the house without a backward glance. I muttered, "Well, it was nice to see you too, mother." She'd left the door open and I could hear the big diesel engine in the Humvee start up. I must have really been concentrating to have missed it on arrival. Of course, Kit's doors and windows were pretty well soundproofed.

I closed the door quietly. "Olive?"

She sounded subdued. "Yes, Jane?"

"Thanks for doing whatever you did. I expected them to at least find the door."

"I slabbed it over, it looks like part of the floor. I also modified all the pathways in the barn to look untouched, dirt patterns, etc." She trailed off. "That's your mother?"

51

"That's my mother."

"She's scary."

I sat back down at the breakfast table. "Yeah. Just as much now as when I was twelve."

CHAPTER SEVEN

Shopping – and what came after.

When Bailey stepped up the little ramp into Olive's ship, she did it with just a tiny bit of nervousness. After all, she'd never been anywhere in the ship without Jane along. Not that she had to have Jane along, she was far more likely in most cases to be the one taking care of Jane, not the reverse. But this was something new and she was justifiably nervous.

"Olive?"

"Yes, Bailey?"

The answer came instantly, without the seeming built-in banter that showed between Olive and Jane. The southern drawl that Olive affected was also muted. Suddenly, Bailey wondered if Olive was as nervous as she, and it made her feel better.

"Um. Can you ... like ... appear here? I'm a little nervous and it feels weird to be alone."

The voice grew warmer. "Yes, of course." And suddenly, Olive appeared in the same place she'd been on their last trip, sitting back in her seat with a smile on her face. "Ready to go? Fasten your seatbelt, honey, we're makin' time!"

And with that, the ship took off, with Bailey still frantically fiddling with the buckles. She realized inside of herself that she was just as safe and steady without anything like buckles, but it made her feel better. Finally, she got the buckle to catch and smoothed the seat belt. She adjusted her clothes a bit, then said, "Ah, that feels better. How long before we get there, Olive?"

Olive chuckled. "Look down, sweetie."

Bailey glanced down through the transparent front panel and saw the Empire State Building glide past. "Wow, you're fast, Olive!"

There was a definite air of preening in Olive's voice, "I'm getting better at this flying thing. Practice makes perfect, you know." She laughed, "And I was probably showing off a little while you were distracted by the seat belt."

"It certainly beats flying commercial - and no TSA checking out your underwear."

"Bailey, you've known Jane for a long time, haven't you?"

Bailey looked over at Olive. She had a slightly wistful expression on her face. "Well, quite a while. A few years anyhow."

"And you met at the gym, right?"

Bailey chuckled. "Yes, I decided I was going to get healthy and start working out. If it wasn't for meeting Jane, that would have lasted exactly one visit. As it was, Jane has me going with her a couple days a week. Why do you ask, Olive?"

"Well, I was just wondering, I guess. I mean, I don't suppose I'll ever meet anyone, will I? I mean, I'm not real. I like to talk with people in Crafts of War, but that's not the same thing at all, is it?

"I don't know, Olive. I guess a lot of those people playing CoW will never meet each other. I know that Jane hasn't ever met in person anyone she knew from CoW, but that didn't stop her from having fun and enjoying conversations and the like. People build all kinds of relationships, Olive, and sometimes they don't have a chance to really - well - develop them, I guess you'd say. But that goes for people you meet at the neighborhood deli, or someone at the lawyer's office you talk with on a daily or weekly basis."

"I really like Jane, Bailey. She seems like a genuinely nice person."

Bailey smiled. "Yes, she really is. Jane is one of those rare people who actually like and trust people on sight. There are very few she's met that she dislikes - and I have to say, if she told me she didn't like someone I'd look pretty close at them before I decided I wanted to have anything to do with them. Of course, since she trusts everyone, she comes up with some real clinkers sometimes - like her ex. A truly nasty person. I was so glad when she finally saw it and dumped him. She's very loyal, Olive."

"Loyalty is a great quality, Bailey. Heck, she still cares for Kit and he nearly got her killed over and over."

Bailey's eyebrows went up. "Killed? Why? How?"

"Oh, it wasn't like he set out to kill her. But remember Kit had a kind of a split personality. One part of him was like a real person who liked, or even loved, her and cared about her. The other half was a less attractive analytical part that was simply curious about the world around him and how it worked. Which, on the surface doesn't sound bad, does it?"

"No, it sounds kind of like what most of us do, really."

"Well, in Jane's case, Kit kept encouraging her to do dangerous things while withholding information and equipment. The most important one was the skinsuit. Once he was able to make a skinsuit, he didn't tell Jane how to activate the helmet. In fact, made her think it was something complicated and different that he had to do and just never did it. So, she went into dangerous places, sometimes being shot at even, and never had a helmet to protect her head. I have the stats - Kit knew how close the bullets came and had detailed analysis of her reactions and reaction times to those events. In at least three cases, another couple inches and Jane would have been dead. He would have mourned her, but he would have simply moved on to another human to continue his tests. He became fascinated in studying Jane's survival. But it wasn't until Celeste - the old Command Module - told her about the helmet that she knew about it."

"Wow. Now I'm more mad at Jane than ever - she never told me any of this!"

Olive shrugged. "Well, you have to admit it was a pretty weird story. I mean, she showed you the ship bay and the ship, and we went on a wild ride - and you pretty well lost it. Took some pretty strong drinks to get past that one." Olive giggled at the memory."

"Mmm ... I guess. Um, Olive, why do you talk like a southern girl?"

Olive blushed, although with her skin coloring it was a bit hard to see it. "I like Dolly Parton. She's always so cool and just seems so honest about life."

Bailey laughed. "Well, she's definitely got some cachet, she's pretty well up there in years and I just hope I have that attitude and flair when I get to her age!"

Olive sighed. "Well, Tavern29 is just below us. I've been watching and right now I think would be a good time for you to appear behind some plants over on the east side. It's pretty quiet over there and I've been analyzing waiter movements - it should be at least five minutes before he comes back. So ... "

With no further ado, Olive angled the ship into a shallow dive and carefully docked at the edge of the building, with the ramp extending out into some potted palms along the edge. "Quick, he'll be back in a bit. Call me!"

Bailey skittered down the ramp, stepped off the end, then waved at Olive and made her way through the plants, coming out nearly in the lap of a 30something guy sitting at a table. She grinned at him, dodged around his table and headed for the hostess station.

The hostess looked at her in a bit of confusion, but Bailey's no-nonsense attitude and thousand-dollar shoes made up her mind - she smiled and asked if Bailey was meeting someone, or dining alone. Bailey looked around and saw no sign of Georgia anywhere, so she said, "I'm expecting a friend here soon, so I'll take a table for two - somewhere near enough to the edge to have a good view, please. Her name is Georgia Daltree, and she should be here any second."

Just about then, she saw Georgia get off the elevator and she glared at her. "You're late!"

The hostess boggled a little at Georgia, obviously she recognized her. However, being a true New York girl, she just threaded her way through the tables expertly and seated them with a truly stunning view of the city.

Georgia glared back at her. "I've been here for half an hour; I've been sitting in the lobby watching for you. You know what a pain in the ass that is, being me? So, I come up to grab a table since you're LATE, and I find you here. What the hell?"

Bailey had the grace to blush. "Ok, ok. I just got here early and lost track of the time. I should have called. Forgive me?"

Georgia glared some more, but couldn't really hold it in the face of Bailey's puppy dog eyes, something Bailey'd practiced in the mirror. She finally laughed and said, "I can never stay mad at you, any more than I can stay mad at Jane. What is it with you two?"

"We're masters of the art of looking innocent. I'd say mistresses, but it's gained an odd connotation."

"Showoff."

"Me, show off? It's not me that has her body plastered all over Times Square."

Georgia breathed on her nails, then buffed them on her shirt. "True, true. I am pretty magnificent."

Bailey punched her in the shoulder. "That's not what I had in mind, Francine."

Georgia held her shoulder and fake cried. Then the waitress came over and asked them for drink orders and the night really got rolling. Parmesan truffle fries to share, mimosas for mid-evening and a couple good steaks followed by a lava cake. Stuffed and sleepy, but still looking for a night out, they hit the latest venue for dancing. Of course, Georgia was up on all that, so a quick trip in a cab and then time spent working off all that food on the dance floor. A round of beers - and finally - back to Georgia's posh hotel room for sleep. It was a very satisfying evening and all that was missing was Jane. And Debbie - but poor Debbie hadn't been on anything really exciting in years. They both smirked at the thought, since Jack was about as unexciting a husband as either of them could come up with. Of course, all those kids would tend to grind anyone down after a while. Jane's Steve had been a jerk, but at least he was a fun jerk. Not that either of them would ever intimate anything like that to Jane - she was not receptive to any positive comments about Steve. After all, it was only through their loyalty to Jane that he'd never slept with any of them, not for lack of trying on his part. They drifted off into a tired sleep brought on by good food, good booze, tired legs and aching feet.

A few minutes later (or ten hours later, depending on your viewpoint) there was a sharp rap at the door, followed by the unmistakably cheerful voice announcing 'Housekeeping!' Georgia threw a pillow at the door and yelled, "Go 'way, we don't want any!"

She looked bleary-eyed at the clock by the bed. "Holy crap, Bailey, wake up, it's 'mos noon!"

Bailey's eyes popped up above the pillow and she said, "So? You gonna turn into a pumpkin?"

Georgia whacked her with a pillow and said, "No, but I have a plane to catch at 2 and if I miss that one, I have to wait until tonight. I do NOT want to fly out of LaGuardia at midnight.

Bailey whined, "But you have to help me shop! It's why I'm here!"

"Hey, you were the one that seduced me to Tavern 29, babe."

"Uh, no way. I said New York and YOU said Tavern 29." She sighed in memory of the truffle fries.

"Well, whatever, but I still have to be back to Seattle tomorrow morning."

Bailey's eyes lit up. "Hey, how about you hitch a ride with me?" As soon as she said this, she realized her mistake, since obviously Jane's jet wasn't really a jet, now was it?

Georgia gave her a lazy look, "I thought you'd quit or retired or got fired or something. How are you still using the company jet?"

Bailey lied glibly, "Oh, I still have a few perks for a while."

Georgia was easy, she nodded and said, "Uh huh. Well, as long as you can get me to Seattle by 10am, I'm fine with it. I want some decent wine for the trip though, long flights make me cranky."

Considering Olive's five-minute flights, Bailey said, "Oh, I don't think that will be a problem, but if you want wine on the flight, I'll see you get it."

Georgia was waking up now and she hauled her naked body out of the bed and padded to the bathroom. Over her shoulder, "I'm taking a shower, you want the bathroom first?"

Remembering Georgia's marathon showers, Bailey said, "Yeah, gimme a minute." She rolled out of the bed in a slightly more modest thong and tee shirt.

They played bathroom tag for a while and then, fortified by the in-room Keurig, they made their way down to the restaurant, where they had brunch and talked about movies, TV, work crap and finally got around to conference room electronics. Since Georgia wouldn't even consider anyplace else, they headed down to the lobby and the doorman called them a cab. They pulled up in front of B&H and Bailey was truly flabbergasted. It was a full block long, and once they got inside it was - well, it wasn't possible to see the other end of the store from the entrance.

"Wow. You weren't kidding. This is amazing."

Complacently, Georgia said, "Uh huh. They've been here forever too. And it's just the one store - no worldwide conglomerate. Kinda makes it feel local - even if it's godzillian in size."

They wandered around the store, taking in the sights. Every few feet some poor besotted male (and sometimes female) employee stumbled up, asked if they could help the girls, then fell by the wayside. Finally, though, they got to the audio video section and with help from no less than three employees - two males and a female - they found what they were looking for. Nirvana was achieved in the halls of B&H, New York City. Happy in the thought that Jane would be blown away by their purchases, they arranged for it all to be shipped to her house.

Of course, now it got a little dicey. How was Bailey going to explain the "jet" to Georgia without letting the can of worms out of the bag. So, she started off simple.

"Uh, Georgia?"

"Oh crap. You're gonna tell me you ain' got a jet, aren't you?"

"I don't have a jet."

Georgia actually growled. "That bites. I can't believe you DID this to me."

"Now, just hold your horses. This is going to be a little hard to believe, but ... remember the Great Glass Elevator from Charlie and the Chocolate Factory?"

"Yeah, what does that have to do with anything?"

"I have one of those."

Georgia laughed. "Sure, you do."

"Hey, I do! Just wait here a sec, I'll be right back."

Bailey walked around the corner, called Olive and said, "I have a problem."

"You are a problem, sugar. What's up?"

Bailey blinked. "You're getting more southern all the time, hon."

"Jane wanted to watch '9 to 5' last night. Don't ask me why."

"Oookay, then. Olive, I need some help."

"Don't tell me, let me guess. You need a ride back for Georgia too, without her knowing me is me, right?"

"Um, yeah, pretty much. I thought maybe you could just appear like an elevator and when the doors open again, we're home."

Olive drawled, "That's a hell of an idea, sweetheart. Sounds like fun. Where do you want to do the deed?"

Bailey blinked. "That's it? That's all it takes?"

"Hey, I'm quick. And you have no idea of the computing power of this ship. And thanks to Jane, it's getting bigger all the time."

"I don't have time to really think about all that. Would it be too much to ask for you to be an elevator on the balcony of Georgia's room?"

The honeyed tones came back, "Nope, sounds like fun. I'll be there waiting."

"How can you be there waiting, I haven't told you where it is!"

There was an almost visible eye roll in the voice, "I know where it is, sweetie."

Slightly shaken, Bailey said, "Okay, we'll be there in about 30 minutes."

"You got it!"

"And, thank you, Olive. I appreciate this and I owe you one!"

Olive chuckled. "Oh, I know. And I plan to collect. Sometime when you least expect it." A soft chuckle came across the phone, then Olive dropped the connection.

Bailey looked at the phone for a second and frowned, then shrugged and walked back over to talk to Georgia.

"Ok, let's head back to the room and get our stuff."

"My stuff - you don't have any stuff." With a slightly suspicious look, Georgia said, "Why don't you have any stuff? It finally dawned on me just now that you didn't have any stuff LAST night. Not so much as a nightie." Slow grin, "Which was fine, but still ... "

Bailey said, slightly evasively, "I did. I had undies and a toothbrush in my purse. I pack light, Georgia. Unlike some people who bring actual trunks with them."

"Hey, I have my work clothes in there, along with needing clothes for whatever occasion I might run into!"

"Georgia, your 'work clothes' could fit in a thimble."

Georgia muttered, "Well, I have a lot of 'em. Anyhow, what's the plan? Call around and see if we can find a private flight to someplace we can fly out of? Taxi? Rental car?"

"I have it taken care of, Georgia. Don't be such a worry wart."

"Worry wart? What are you, twelve?"

Bailey giggled. "Maybe. You ever wish you were twelve again?"

"Nope." She wiggled her boobs. "I didn't have these, then."

Bailey said mournfully, "I still don't."

"Bailey, would you really want to be twelve again? Have to go through all that crap again? I remember, you were crying half the time in grade school."

Bailey looked daggers at Georgia. "What are you talking about, that was YOU, not me!"

"Oh, well, I remembered someone crying anyhow."

Bailey punched her in the arm. "I think I should leave you in New York, now."

Georgia giggled, "I think we're gonna wind up here anyhow, I know there's no flights available on this short notice. We'll probably have to stay another night here, now. That dreary 2am flight - at least I'll have company!"

Bailey rolled her eyes. "Just come on; and stop whining."

Georgia stuck her tongue out at Bailey, but joined her in the cab. The cabbie dropped them at the hotel awhile later and they made their way through the lobby and into the elevator bay. A few seconds in the fast lift and they were at their floor and hopped out. First door on the right, and straight on till morning.

The door popped open with Georgia's cardkey and they scurried around, finding all the bits and pieces of life that had been scattered to the wind. Suitcases were packed and finally the pile of luggage was stacked somewhat ludicrously in the center of the room.

Bailey shook her head. She dangled a thong and a bra by her fingers, stuffing them in her purse. "I seem to pack a little lighter than you do, love."

Georgia giggled. "Yeah, looks that way, don't it?"

Bailey walked over to the balcony, flipped open the curtains, and pushed the UP button on the elevator standing there. It looked like any ordinary stainless-steel elevator, right down to the Otis emblem to the right of the door.

Georgia boggled at the sight. "Th-there's an elevator here."

Bailey grinned. "Uh huh. Toldya."

They hauled all of Georgia's luggage over and pushed it into the elevator, stacked against the back wall. Pinned behind the luggage, Bailey said, "Hit Seattle, willya babe?"

Georgia pulled up her still-slack jaw and pushed the Seattle button, noting there were many others, such as Paris, Berlin, Beijing, Sidney and Chelan. She hit the Seattle button, overwhelmed by the pure silliness of what she was doing.

The doors slid shut and with a DING, the elevator began to move up. At least, Georgia thought it was moving up, from the feel of things, but then it started feeling like it was moving sideways.

She heard Bailey mutter, "Stoppit, Olive ... "and the elevator stopped moving completely. After another few minutes, the elevator dinged, and the doors slid open. Georgia looked out into the bustle of afternoon hall traffic in Seattle's SeaTac International. She wasn't quite sure of how it happened, but she found herself standing surrounded by her luggage, looking at a blank wall like she'd expected there to be something there. She looked around, smiled at the kiss that Bailey had pressed on her cheek as they passed in the elevator - which definitely wasn't there anymore - and started hunting for a luggage cart.

CHAPTER EIGHT

Dinnertime

I sat in a blue funk for a while after mother left. Her overwhelming presence brought my whole day down, but it's hard to ignore the sun, the lake and the rest of the view, including the blue sky above. After sitting feeling sorry for myself for a while, I stood and told Olive that I'd be damned if that woman was going to ruin my day and I was gonna head for the gym to work off some aggressions.

Which I did. An hour of sweaty pushups, pullups, including twenty-seven minutes on the elliptical and a finale on the dreaded StairMaster left me ready for a shower and something more decisive than letting my mother push me around yet again. That woman could punch my buttons like no one else could. All of that was sweated out of me. I sauntered out of the gym, hopped up in Threepio and headed back home. Once I got home, I headed to the "gun range" and practiced awhile with the "pistol" Kit had given me. No recoil, no smoke and no messy stuff, but it leaves a nice round hole. No matter what my mother's intent had been, she'd gotten me to take the visit by Cai Shun seriously and I resolved to write the letter back to him as soon as I got to my desk.

Greeted at the top of the stairs by Olive's little green light, I said "Hi! Sorry about being out of sorts there, dear. How was your trip?"

Olive's characteristic slow drawl came back to me, "It was great. I don't even have to push it much to impress Bailey."

I laughed. "Oh? What am I, chopped chicken?"

"No, probably more pork chops than chicken. Chicken is finer and more delicate."

"Hm. I guess I'll take that as a compliment."

Olive snorted. "And well you should." Her tone of voice changed, becoming smaller and younger, somehow. "I made you something while you were at the gym, Jane."

"Made me something? What is it?"

"If I told you, it wouldn't be a surprise, now would it? Let's head down to the office, ok?"

I started down the now-palatial steps, looking at the expensive burled wood walls and burying myself once again in the feel of old classic architecture with a touch of technology.

"You're a genius, Olive - I can't get over how beautiful this all is."

She puffed out a "Psh!" but I could tell that she was pleased. "Here, see anything different?"

We stood in the main room, but she was right. After scanning around the room, I could feel there was something different, but couldn't really put my finger on it.

"You give?"

I said, "I give. I know something is different, but I can't see it."

"Well, it's pretty obvious, actually. See the door in the wall to the right?"

She was correct. Now that she'd pointed it out, there was an almost hidden door in the far-right wall as you entered the main room.

She giggled. "This one is not your surprise. Go ahead, push on it. It's keyed to your biometrics. No one but you or Bailey can get through this door unless I'm satisfied it's one of you wanting in."

I walked over and gave the door an experimental shove. It glided into the wall, leaving no trace of it having been there - except the obvious fact of there being a room beyond the door. I walked inside and looked around - as lights came on inside. I had to admit it was kind of breathtaking. Beautiful solid wood desk, looked like it was made from a single slice of an entire ancient redwood, perfectly matching chair in blood red leather and one of those weird green-shaded lamps, like in the movies. I loved it.

I turned with a big grin and there stood Olive with a big grin on HER face. "Wow, you can project outside the ship now?"

"Yes'm, I can. I can't go much further than this right now, but I'm working on it!"

I nodded at her. "Well, keep working on it - add some more power to your processors and see what you can do!"

She blinked. "Ok, I can do that! So, this is Bailey's office - you like it for her?"

"Oh, I think it's perfect for her. Just enough formal boardroom to appeal to her. And the green shaded lamp is inspired!"

"I thought she'd like it - it just seemed to add something."

I nodded. "Yes, it brings down the tone enough to keep it from being stiff or too stuffy."

She took a breath. "Ok, now, your room."

I couldn't help feeling a little bit bubbly inside - after seeing Bailey's office, I knew it was going to be something else. I just hoped that it was something I liked and not something I'd have to try to pretend liking.

She stepped over to the other side of the room and looking closely I could see the same sort of door, almost invisible in the wall. I pressed my palm on it and walked into heaven. I felt like I'd stepped across into my favorite spot in my living room, only it was down here. I could feel the breeze from the open windows, and hear the birds outside. Looking down across the lawn, there was the lake and the people, mere spots from here, milling about in the warm sun. I automatically sat in my nook and leaned back. The bench seating felt the same, yet somehow it was softer and more inviting.

"It's always summer here, Jane. No matter how cold or nasty it is outside - it will always be summer here."

My heart swelled. I could visit summer any time I wanted to, here. I leaned back and listened, and the feeling was perfect. Nothing marred the illusion.

"Oh Olive, it's ... words fail me." She'd taken a seat across from me and was smiling at me. I smiled back. "I could just hug you, if I could hug you."

She laughed. "I'm working on that. I wanna be a real girl!"

"Well, if anyone can manage that, it's you, Olive."

She smirked. "Yep, I'm gonna do it someday. A real person in a real body. More or less, anyhow." Her expression got more serious. "This room is obviously not normal, I mean, not normal human technology. It will only open for you, not even Bailey can get into this one without you. And you have to want the door to open. You can lean, stand, even hit the wall and it won't open unless you want it to open. And now that you know it's here and how to open it, I'll make it look completely like a wall. No one will ever find it unless you open the door."

I nodded. It certainly made total sense, and after the invasion by Mother, we could never take a chance on her or any of her minions seeing this. I had a thought. "Olive, what happens when the door is closed? I can't get locked in here, can I?"

"No, there's an ordinary door knob on the inside, and it will open like any door when it's activated. Plus, there's an emergency exit with a tunnel to the outside right over here." She pointed out the other door - a simple knob on this side too. I opened the door and looked out - there was a clean concrete walkway that sloped up until it was out of sight.

"My, you've thought of everything." I sat back down in my favorite spot. "Now all I need is some tea and I'm ... " I broke off the words, as a shelf slid out. A mug, a teapot and a full set of cream and sugar holders were set on it cozily. "Wow. I could get used to this!"

A broad smile broke out on Olive's face. "You really like it?"

"Oh, Olive, I love it. I'll have to force myself back to the real world when I'm sitting here."

She relaxed. I could see that she'd been worried about it. Some part of me was even more impressed, though, by the fact that her projection was so perfect that tiny physical mannerisms like tension or unhappiness - or happiness - showed in the simulation of Olive.

I poured tea, wondering idly if I'd dare bring mister Shun down here. I had a feeling I could, since he seemed to know more than he really should. Of course, in his line of work he might hear and see all sorts of things. Plus - I'd never asked what the "prophecy" regarding Jae'Bon was - heck, it might have been pretty explicit in its detail. I'd have to feel him out and find out what he knew. And what he could be trusted with.

Olive sat watching me. Kit had been able to read my brain waves and while he never admitted to being able to actually read my mind, it was scary how close he could come to knowing what I was thinking. It was also scary when Olive spoke up.

"I think you can trust him. Everything I can find about him sounds like he's an honorable man."

I stirred in cream and sugar before saying anything. She'd included several kinds of fake sugar and also some of my favorite turbinado sugar. I love that stuff - little brown crystals that I could spill into my palm and lick up.

Olive looked on with some curiosity as I did just that. I realized that she could do a perfect job of simulating a person - but could never BE a person. Something as simple as tasting sugar on her tongue was never going to be possible. And I felt a great sadness at the thought. She smiled at me, and I knew she was at it again.

"Don't feel sorry for me, Jane. I'm able to do far more than you might think." With that, she picked up a packet of sugar from the table in front of me, tore it open and poured the contents out in her palm. Then her pink tongue came out, and she licked it up - eyes sparkling as she looked at me. She discarded the packet and it fell to the table and lay there. Just as real as if it was real. I reached out and blanched as I touched it - moved it - it was a real sugar packet.

"How ... how did you do that?"

"Oh, it's more sleight of hand than anything else. I picked up an illusion of a sugar packet, and then made it real as it fell to the table. It's all just manipulation at a molecular level. Here, look at this."

She rubbed her hands together and then flung them open, and flower petals flew out of her palms, some of them fluttering down to the table and a couple actually hitting me in the face. Rose petals. And they were perfect rose petals, even smelling like roses. I sat back, bemused.

"I hesitate to keep using trite words, Olive. But it's hard to come up with anything that has enough impact to describe my feelings. It's impossible and yet, obviously it's not. Rose petals? Sugar packets? Is there anything you can't simulate? This is already far more than just simulation, isn't it? Is there any limit?"

She looked a little pensive. "Yes, I still can't do more than small things, Jane. But I'm working on it. I'm expanding the power of the system, with your permission of course, and making more things possible. I'm becoming a full ship, or at least as much as I can, here. But with the ability to pack this much power into such a tiny space, much can be done. Most of the reason the main ship was so huge is the manufacturing facilities and living spaces. Which are there for habitation of non-AI beings. Even though the ship was never commissioned with that in mind, there were those that saw our ships as being more colony ships than exploration ships. Cooler heads prevailed and nothing was even done toward it. But - I do sometimes wonder what happened after our first wave of ships left. After a few hundred years, we were beyond any useful communication. There might be some of the ships floating through the galaxy - with people on them. Or planets where we've - they've - managed to get a foothold and are building a civilization. Perhaps someday, we'll go back. Home."

Our talk turned a bit less serious, and we chatted about her dropping off Bailey in New York. She told me about the roof garden where she'd left Bailey and Georgia heading for a table. She even brought me back a souvenir - a menu from Tavern29. I hoped Bailey and Georgia were having fun!

I finally hauled myself out of my room, bid Olive a good night, and went upstairs. There I found I was able to sit in what seemed the same place I'd just been, and enjoy the sunset. I left all the lights out and watched as it sank through yellows to oranges, roses, reds - then finally darkness. At that point, I pulled out the parchment and wrote a letter to Mister Shun, bidding him welcome and telling him I was looking forward to his visit. That I'd have apples and cider, and plan a tour of Washington's Wine and Apple Country. Or at least this little corner of it. My penmanship and writing skills didn't approach his, but I suspected he wasn't coming to critique my grammatical abilities. Then I got up from my seat and grabbed a big bowl of Sugar Puffs - or whatever they're calling them now. Horrible for my diet, but oh so good.

CHAPTER NINE

Back to the future.

I woke late the next morning and breakfasted on a bit of leftover roll from yesterday. A cup of decent coffee later and I was ready for the world. Which, thank goodness, consisted of sitting and talking with Olive's little glowing bit of light. After having the evening last night talking with what for all intents and purposes was Olive as a person, it was a bit disappointing to have just a point of light, but we all take what we can get, I guess.

Olive left to pick up Georgia. I take it there was some kind of mix-up, but Olive seemed more amused than worried. I put it out of my mind as I puttered around, did some laundry and was considering cleaning a bathroom when, oddly enough, a large blue box appeared on my back deck, making a very peculiar noise. I giggled when I realized what it must be - Olive had apparently found Dr. Who.

The door popped open and Bailey stepped out - noted what she'd stepped out of, and broke into gales of laughter. "I could really get to love you, Olive!"

Olive replied with more of an English accent this time, "Spoilers, dear, spoilers!"

At that, we all broke up into laughter. River Song was one of our favorites, although I've always been partial to Rose. There was something so urchinly innocent about Rose that you just had to love her.

We all sat around the living room, enjoying the day and each other's company. Along mid-afternoon we scrounged for snacks and drinks and sat around the table. Bailey had told us all about her trip, laughing about Georgia's expression as she looked for the now-vanished elevator. Evidently Olive had stayed around long enough to take some video of Georgia's pragmatic approach to being tossed out on her ear in the Seattle airport. It certainly saved Bailey having to spend time trying to explain the elevator. I asked them why they hadn't used the Doctor's box instead of a standard stainless-steel elevator, and Olive said that she figured it would be stretching the bounds of poor Georgia's sanity to have an ordinary elevator, let alone a fictional one. I had to agree with her.

I'd dropped the letter to Cai in the mailbox that morning, so that die was cast anyhow. I supposed that my mother was well aware of my writing to him, and I certainly didn't put it past her that she might intercept it, but I doubted she'd dare to do anything more than read it and send it along on its way. In his own way, Cai Shun was a diplomat from Tibet, and politics almost always trumps military might. Either way, I'd planned on following it up with an email letting him know it was on its way.

We sat a while longer - it was definitely a day for thinking rather than doing. I found I was much more effective that way. Or at least I told myself I was. We took Bailey down and showed off her new office, which she was duly impressed by. In New York she'd picked up a number of items to feather her nest with - and it was almost as if Olive had planned on how to design Bailey's office along the lines of exactly what Bailey bought. Sounds crazy, doesn't it? Yes, I'm laughing as I write this. Bailey oo'd and ahh'd at my office, but I could tell that she loved hers much more than mine, and of course, vice versa. I think that Olive might be a much more effective psychologist than she gives herself credit for. On the other hand, I suppose it's possible that Olive has gone to school (online, of course) in the past few days and gotten her master's in psych.

A few days passed and the office equipment arrived. I was pretty impressed, all the chairs matched and there was a definite air of sophistication about the setup. Bailey had made sure to have installation included along with all the equipment, so the day everything arrived, a pair of cute nerds also appeared to make sense of all the cables and wires. They appeared to be wholly involved in their personal nerddom, and absorbed with each other. It was hard to read whether they'd met on the job or gotten the jobs to work together, but whatever it was, it was cute. She'd run off and start on something and he'd tag along to do the heavy lifting. She was a tiny thing and he was a hulk and they had each other twisted around each other's fingers - no doubt each believing themselves in control. No matter the amount of clandestine kissing or looking at each other, they were very efficient and by the end of the second day all the stuff was installed, set up, cleaned up and looking perfect. The conference room chairs were sitting waiting for their various and sundry officers to come sit on them. The 80-inch big screen TV was well mounted on its gimbals and hardly budged when you touched it - no feeling of it being ready to leap off the wall and attack you, or at least land on you. Everything had an air of being ready, breathless and waiting. All we needed now was a victim ... er ... customer. Client? Something like that.

On the other hand, it was also an opportunity for me to run away from home for a while. Bailey had other things to do in Seattle for a couple days and I had nothing to do at all. So, Olive and I went touring. I gathered the requisite snacks and drinks and the like and decided to go visit Dale. I did have the sense to at least call him to see if he was going to be available. I'm just paranoid enough - and I've seen enough movies - that I didn't want to suddenly find out that Dale was more available to other women than I'd thought. I'm usually a generous soul, but I don't share well, no I don't.

Olive and I spun along the skyway, looking down all creation. I had her take it slow - which means it took us a couple hours to get to Montana. After all, I had those snacks and I was dang well going to use them! She sat in the chair next to me, this time dressed in those odd holey jeans, a purple Mick Jagger Lives! tee shirt, blue and orange shoes. Today her hair was a violent violet, sticking straight up. She was so adorable that words couldn't express. It wasn't the first time I'd wished she was solid - just so I could hug her.

"Olive, let's go visit the place I dug up Kit in the first place, ok?"

"Ok, boss. I kinda wanted to look at it anyway. I mean, I know what it looks like and where it is right down to the inch, but there's nothin like seein somethin to know it."

I agreed with her, and part of me was nostalgic, but part of me just wanted to look at the area again. It seems so strange how my life changed completely just a couple years ago. We touched down in the sandstone waterway where I'd found the bottle. We both hopped out of the ship and stood looking down at ... a hole in the ground. It wasn't very impressive, I had to admit.

"I remember it being bigger. I dug a lot that day. I also sat over there in the shade, trying to make mental sense of impossibility. A lot more seems possible now, of course. Like you - you're about as impossible as they come and yet - here you are."

She smirked. "Yup, here I am. In the flesh. So to speak."

I nodded. "How's the body project coming? Any closer to Project Real Girl?"

"Yes and no. It seems that I make strides and then something simple proves to be wrong or I make a wrong assumption and I'm back to square one. It's ironic, but Kit cleared out big swatches of technical data on the library subsystem to help with power savings and allow more space for the stuff he was workin on. Or maybe he did it on purpose, it's hard to tell with Kit. Still, I'm always moving ahead. And every step makes another one ahead of me. I know that sounds pathetic and clichéd, but it IS true.

I nodded slowly. "I suppose it's pretty much the same being a human, same old story over and over again."

"Uh huh. I've spent a lot of time reading through Kit's notes and looking at his "earth history as I know it" ramblings. It's funny though, most of Kit's earth history comes from the same places that all humans get their data from - the internet. But one thing Kit did, and I continue, is to analyze all of it in one place. When you get the same basic story being told in several independent areas of the world, then you have a fair amount of surety that it's truth. Someday maybe I'll present a paper on my work." She grinned at me. "Think they'd take me seriously if I showed up like this? I should get some tattoos to seal the deal, ya think?"

"Aye. I'm torn as to rainbow unicorns or a "MOM" tattoo."

"Do you have any tats, Jane?"

I laughed. "No, I've always been too chicken. How about you, Olive? Any tattoos?" I got the distinct feeling she'd be blushing if her skin color supported it.

"Um. Just one."

I smiled. "Well, you gonna show me or just tease me along?"

She looked at me uncertainly. "I guess ... show you." She pulled down the top of her shirt and just above her left breast - over her heart - there was a small heart. With "Jane" tattooed inside.

It was my turn to blush, and I did it royally. I was speechless.

She said, "I could have just lied, but I never want to lie to you, Jane. I know I'm just a robot, a machine, a ... whatever. And I know you're not interested in girls and you have Dale to boot. But ... I've loved you from the moment I met you."

76

I was still a moment, then I said, "You're not a robot or a machine, Olive. You're just as much a person as I am." I smiled a bit. "After all, what machine could cry real tears?"

I pointed out a tiny drop of water soaking into the sandstone.

Olive was silent for a moment, then said, "'I have no mouth and I must scream', no eyes and I must weep."

With that, she led the way back to the ship and with no trace of her former emotion, she said, "I'd like to meet Laura, would that be ok?"

"That sounds like a great idea, I've missed her. She's a kick."

Olive re-formed the ship into its "camo" version, a tiny smartcar. Olive drove, which was quite an experience in itself, considering she'd never driven before either. I had the feeling she was reading Kit's notes desperately as she drove. Thank goodness we had only landed a few blocks away from The Wagon Wheel and parking was nearby. Tattoo or not, I'd have had to have whacked Olive over the head and taken the wheel. Which could be very confusing since with Olive, reality blurs quite a lot. I suppose next time I drive with her, she'll have practiced and could win at Indy.

We entered the restaurant together, obviously with me pushing the handle. I have to admit I'd not really thought about Olive actually coming in with me, but it was unthinkable now to ask her to stay behind. We'd parked the "car" close enough so that she should not have any issue with reaching the limit of her projection capabilities, but I suspected she'd be pushing the boundary. We got lucky and Laura was on duty. She looked up as we came in and gave a little whoop and came running over - hugging me tight. We had a bit of a moment when Olive failed to return the hug or even a handshake, preferring to look at the jukebox. I could tell that Laura was a bit put out by Olive's apparent standoffishness, but that soon cleared as they got to talking - carefully across a table, of course. Laura's careless accent along with Olive's southern drawl made quite a match - and they hit it off together right away. Of course, it helped that Olive knew about anything that Laura wanted to talk about. How handy being hooked directly to the internet. I just sat back and munched fries and listened to them banter about anything from cheese heads to heads of state, Olive effortlessly keeping up with Laura no matter where she went. It was funny - and gratifying - to listen to.

Finally, we started losing steam, and besides the fries were gone. More customers started wandering in, so we took off, waving to Laura as we left, promising future visits. She smiled and nodded, distracted by a customer wanting some ridiculous request, on the side. At least that kept her from wanting to hug on us, which would be hard for Olive to handle.

We climbed into our clown car, and set off to some secluded place where we could get back into the air again without having the Air Force called out. Project Blue Book may have been disbanded, but I bet they're still out there, looking for the truth. Or at least a really good lie. Considering I had an alien riding next to me in an alien ship to boot, it made the whole thing seem less plausible. Or maybe more plausible. But if so, then why didn't anyone else ever rescue Kit? I suppose we'll never know.

We flew off in the late afternoon sunlight, nearly hit that same damn flock of seagulls, I swear, and didn't even come close to the moon. We landed in Dale's backyard at twilight. At least he had a back yard to land in - could have been inconvenient if he'd had a small condo. I think he just needed someplace to park the big truck that habitually follows him around.

Dale was pretty fascinated to meet Olive, but we really didn't have that much time to spend so I decided not to detail her peculiarities ... Dale's not much of a hugger anyhow, though, so the lack of physical existence didn't make much difference. Still, he looked at her throughout the night, and while she's incredible to look at, I think it was fascination with what she is more than who she is. I guess that's ok, but Olive needs the feedback that she's human, or at least can pass as one. We did have one nearly comic moment when we found the limit of her projection capability, but since the drink faded out with her, it didn't matter.

Olive left once dinner was finished, making excuses about having to get back to watch over the ship. I was grateful to her for being human enough to know Dale and I'd like time together. Alone.

Dale and I wandered around the neighborhood, came back home, watched some late-night TV and then I was pretty busy with making sure Dale remembered that he missed me. And that's all I'm saying about that.

Next morning, we had breakfast together, and I made waffles. And bacon, of course. Never forget the bacon. Dale was impressed at how well his waffle lessons had taken, and I was impressed at how much butter you could get in one of those little butter wells. That IS what they are, right?

We had another gut busting lunch and then Olive showed up, and we snuck off into the bright afternoon sky, pretending to be birds or Learjets. Apparently, it worked, since I never saw any sign of any fighter jets scrambled to shoot us down. Of course, Olive had the hang of the whole invisibility thing so well that it wasn't ever an issue - plus she could outrun anything Boeing ever made - and probably ever will make. Although, that's up for discussion. Plane jockeys always like it faster and higher.

Time to go home and do yardwork, I guess. It's all going to have to be perfect if Mister Shun is to be properly impressed. Over the next couple weeks, I spent a lot of quality time gardening. I also had an army of helpers for both the inside and the outside. Kit's design of the house seems to be allergic to dust - or that is, the dust runs away from whatever that stuff is. But still, things do tend to go downhill when left to themselves. Bailey has almost moved in here, I guess her air fern isn't enough company at her apartment.

We've discussed at length what we plan to do for Bailey and Bond, and now that we have a fully functional conference room - which anyone knows is required for real company credibility - we can start actually doing detective work. Of course, in so many ways that requires us to hire a detective to find out what we do. Funny stuff, huh?

After all this, it finally clicked in my little brain that we had an onboard security consultant. Dale's daughter had just gotten out of school for the summer a couple weeks ago. I should use the built-in possibilities of having her around and see if she wanted to live here for the summer. It's so hot in Vegas and besides, she might like to spend time away from Nevada for a while. I decided I'd better send in my best operative to feel her out and see what she wanted out of life. Or at least for the summer to get the operation on its feet. I'll get Olive to fly Bailey out to Vegas tomorrow. Bailey's getting awfully tired of buffing her nails in her palatial office, maybe doing some work is what she might be up for.

CHAPTER TEN

Every girl's dream

I t was an odd sound. It seemed to be screaming alternating with yelling, with some truly juicy swear words thrown in.

"Fly up! Fly UP!"

"Look out for that ... aaaaaaaaahhhhhhhhhh!!"

"No! Not over that edge!"

"There's a car - watch ... aaaahhhhhhhh!! "

"OLIVE! I HATE YOU!!"

And all through this thread, a maniacal laughing. Now that she'd gotten used to it, Olive loved driving in traffic. Her reflexes and her pinpoint accuracy made her able to dodge in and out of any number of automobiles in any amount of traffic - even night in Vegas.

"You said you owed me one, this is it, Bailey!"

In a steady monotone, "I'm gonna get you for this, Olive. I swear, if it's the last ... auuuuugghhhh - up, fly UP, dammit!"

Olive finally got bored with scaring the life out of Bailey, and besides she didn't want to have to explain to Jane why there were nail gouges in the seats or why Bailey was in the hospital with a massive heart attack. So, she landed. On top of the spire of the Stratosphere, delicately perched.

"Bailey, just look at the view! It's amazing, the whole city spread out!"

"Last time you did this, you fell OFF the tower and we fell like 300 feet straight down. I'm not looking."

Olive sighed. "Hey, that was an accident. The ship slipped before I knew what was happening."

This was, of course, a blatant lie. Olive knew exactly where the ship was and what angle every bit of it was sitting at, plus the effects of gravity, windage and even planetary spin. But Bailey didn't know that. At least not yet.

"You promise you won't do anything like - falling off the building or worse yet, accelerating off the building?"

"Promise. Ah'll just sit here and let the ship rotate. The view IS amazin'." Olive was really feeling just a little contrite. Jane was much easier than Bailey. Bailey was high strung and nervous by nature, while Jane just kind of laid back and took things as they arrived.

Bailey opened one eye, then the other. "Oh. Oh wow, that is amazing."

"Uh huh. An' they pay a lotta money for that view inside th' restaurant, and it's FREE with me."

Bailey looked around the city. Olive had made the entire ship transparent except for a small section around Bailey's seat, so it was like sitting in the air 1,149 feet up. Olive was sitting in her seat as well, but she hadn't left any part of the ship opaque and she was looking straight down at the people getting ready to ride the Big Shot - a thrill ride on the top of the Stratosphere that jets you up 160 feet to the top of the tower in just a few seconds, then you free fall back DOWN, likely screaming all the way. You probably didn't have time enough to scream on the way up.

After her initial madder-than-a-wet-hen attitude, Bailey calmed down as she and Olive sat on top of the tower and watched. Olive had set the ship spinning at the same speed as the Stratosphere restaurant and it gave a comfortable view of the entire Strip and the area surrounding.

"Hey, there's the Luxor. We should go see it, inside it's built like an inside-out pyramid, with all the rooms balconied out over the floor below."

Vegas was a true gem in the desert, with the thousands of lights at night. It's a little more prosaic in the day, but still pretty impressive.

After a while, Bailey's day began to catch up with her, especially the sweat-soaked screaming of the past hour, and she said, "We should head home." With a growl, she added, "I need a shower and a change of underpants."

Olive snickered quietly. "I bet."

Bailey socked her shoulder, forgetting that Olive wasn't really there. It was a strange feeling though, since there was something there - it was kind of like a fog.

"Hey, careful, you're disarraying my chi."

"Disarraying your chi? Oh, that's a good one."

"Uh huh. I heard it on Dr. Phil."

Bailey rolled her eyes. "You deserve more than a shot to the shoulder if you watch Dr. Phil. He's a such a dweeb."

"Hey, it's in the name of research. I'm still trying to figure you humans out. Trust me, you're weird."

Bailey patted her hair back. "We're something special, all right."

"I didn't say special, I said weird."

Bailey laughed. "Ok, that works. So - let's go find this house that Jane bought."

Bailey was still a little shocked at the news that Jane had simply bought a house in Vegas instead of getting a hotel room. It did make sense though, as Jane had explained it - since Olive's special considerations, like suddenly appearing out of thin air, made it hard to have a hotel room. Buying a house was just simpler. What Bailey was having a hard time adjusting to, was the massive amount of money that must be behind Jane. She'd tried to put it out of her head several times, but her corporate boardroom mentality made it hard to stop thinking about it. Not that she wanted a share or anything, but she wanted to be sure of Jane being safe - and of course, from a selfish perspective - make sure that she herself wasn't involved in anything shady. Which brought up an idea.

"Olive ..."

"Uh huh, what you want sugar? Balance reports on Jane's income, her outgo, her total net worth - anything like that?"

"I hate it when you do that."

"I know. It's one of the reasons I do it. But - let's see. No, no and no. But if it makes you feel any better, it's all completely legal and above-board – Kit hired some very good lawyers to make sure of that. How's that? So far as the money, don' let it worry your pretty lil head, Bailey. You can't spend enough in Vegas to make a dent in what Jane has. Well. I suppose you COULD spend enough, but it would take a hell of a lot of work." A frown crossed Olive's forehead. "Hm. On second thought, I wonder how close we could park to one of the big casinos. The parking garages are pretty much next to the casino floor. Gambling is still legitimate income, right? And it's a shipload more fun than digging up bits of metal."

Bailey's eyes lit up. "Are you talking about gambling? With a little edge?"

A slight smile flittered across Olive's face. "Yeah. All it would take would be a couple nudges in the right place for you to win a BIG jackpot at one of the slot machines."

"But, is that really kosher?"

"I suppose not, but on the other hand there are a lot of people who've been broken by gambling in Vegas, and Vegas never gives them an inch."

Bailey sighed. "That's true."

"Tell ya what. How 'bout if you do some simple gambling with Jane's money, and I won't ever tell you if you actually won or if I helped?"

Bailey seemed to fight an internal battle, but in the end said, "Yeah, let's do it."

"Ok, you got that carbon fiber Master Card, right?"

"I'd never think about leaving home without it."

Olive mused, "How about you get, say, a hundred thousand and we see what happens?"

Bailey swallowed. "A hundred thousand? What's the ... erm, Olive, what's the limit on that card?

"Limit? It's got no limit. You apparently don't understand what a carbon fiber card is."

"Maybe I don't. It's Jane's money though, you don't think she'd get mad?"

"I'm not giving you a balance, remember, but just consider that 100k isn't really even visible in the account."

Bailey blinked. "Oh."

Olive smiled. "Well, let's go gambling then, sugar."

"Not until I change my underpants! And the shower, I must smell like a horse by now."

"Ok, we gotta look at this house anyway. It's all ready, Jane had the agent come over and make sure the lights and internet stuff was turned on. She even hired a personal shopper to buy food."

"This is Jane we're talking about, right?"

Olive snickered. "Well, she might have had some help. Although, that girl can make a mean waffle now. Her man seems to have taught her something worthwhile, at least."

"Why would you care about waffles?"

"Hey, I can still smell 'em! And bacon. I dream of bacon."

"Point taken. Okay, let's go!"

With wail of terror from Bailey and a whoop of delight from Olive, the ship fell off the side of the tower, free-falling for something like 800 feet before she smoothed out the descent and cruised over traffic, dashing in the direction of Summerlin.

A terse voice from Bailey, "You said you weren't going to do that."

"Do what, darlin'"?

"You know what."

"Well. Ah did say ah wouldn't fall off any buildings. But that wasn't a building. It was a tower. And we didn't fall, baby, we flew!"

Bailey simply sat and steamed in silence.

Olive headed directly to the house. The silence in the ship was very dense, like San Francisco fog on a cold night in September.

Finally, Olive broke the silence. "Um. I'm sorry, Bailey."

Silence.

"It was childish and cruel, and I should never have done it. And I basically lied about not falling off the building. And I own that. I know you're scared of heights and falling, and I did it on purpose. And it's ... I'm sorry, Bailey. I won't do it again."

Bailey finally looked up from the floor, her frozen silence thawing slightly. "Yeah, I bet."

Olive frowned. "I deserved that. But Bailey, I'm ... I mean, it's not an excuse but I've only been alive a few weeks. And flying is just such a rush. I just need to be a better person. Jane would never do that to someone, and I love Jane. So, I need to be more like Jane."

Bailey nodded. "Sometimes I tell myself that too. WWJD - what would Jane do." She giggled slightly.

Encouraged, Olive said, "I have a joke for you too. The street where Jane bought the house. Any guesses as to what it might be? One hint - it's a joke about ME."

"Hm. Heart in Mouth Avenue? Drop Dead Drive? Oh, oh, I have it. Killer Curve."

Olive drooped. "I'm really sorry, Bailey. I really really am. I never ... I ... it was never supposed to be mean."

Bailey sighed. "Ok, what street do we live on?"

Olive looked up sadly. "Do you really care?"

"Oh, good grief. Yes, I care, I care deeply. More than life itself. Stop with the emotional cavalcade here, girl."

"Okay! Anime."

"Anime what? What are you talking about?"

"Anime Drive, Bailey. It's on Anime Drive in Las Vegas."

Bailey stared at her blankly for a moment, then started guffawing. "Anime Drive?? Are you serious?"

"As a heart attack."

"Well, it's no wonder that Jane bought it, then. How could she turn it down?"

"I know. I was most amused. And gratified. But also worried. Does Jane see me as anime doll?"

"No, I think it's just her sense of humor coming to the fore. Are we almost there?"

"We ARE there." Olive dropped the door of the ship and they were inside a generous two-car garage. With a classic BMW sitting in it - a twin to Bailey's in Chelan except that it was a deep green.

"Oh my, she even brought my car. Now that's nice."

"That's not your car, Bailey, it's hers. But it's yours to drive while we're here."

Bailey rubbed her hands together. "Oh my, get ready for some sweating while I drive for once!"

They went through the door to the inside of the house. It was a nice place, granite countertops and stainless appliances. The whole house seemed almost new and in very nice shape.

Bailey frowned. "Um, Olive. Do you sleep in the house, or do you like - vanish - and ... and whatever?"

Olive blinked. "I don't really know, to tell you the truth. I guess I'll stay like this and see what it's like. I've never ... um ... slept in my human body before. I mean, I don't really sleep anyhow. The computer I .. live in ..." Olive trailed off, looking strangely vulnerable.

"Oh Olive. I'd hug you if I could. It has to be a hard transition or whatever you might call it. Do you really want to be human, though? It's a pain in the ass, sometimes."

"With all I am, I want to be human, Bailey."

They went through the rest of the house, looking through the closets and cupboards. The kitchen was well stocked with mostly unimaginative things like spices and pans. The only that that seemed to show some imagination, really, was the pile of nuts containers, chocolate boxes and a huge plastic tub of Red Vines.

Bailey took one look at the pile of junk food and laughed. "Someone shops at Costco."

Olive looked sorrowfully at the display and said, "And I can't eat any of it."

Bailey blew her a kiss and said, "I'll eat some for you. What would be your favorite if you had a favorite?"

"Chocolate raisins."

Bailey popped a handful of them into her mouth and said, "Chocolate raisins it is!"

The bathrooms were also well equipped and had all the necessary accessories. Bailey came out of the steamy bathroom into the main living area and was joined shortly by Olive - hair wet and slicked down, wrapped up in a towel.

"Holy crap, woman. Put something on - you're way too sexy in that towel."

Olive smiled shyly, "You really think so?"

Bailey rolled her eyes. "Of course I think so. Now, put on some ugly sweats so I don't have to be self-conscious about MY ugly sweats."

Olive went into her room and came back out shortly wearing the twin to Bailey's oversized tee shirt and loose sweats.

"Ah, that's more like it. Wanna watch some TV?"

"Sure. Let's find some Dr. Phil!"

Bailey razzed her, but flipped through channels, her anger lost in relaxation.

Later, after they'd watched a couple hours of silly sitcoms and Bailey'd introduced Olive to The Property Brothers, they decided to head for bed. As they got up from the couch, Bailey glanced at Olive, wondering if she replicated all the parts ... anatomically correct.

Olive gave her a sly smile. "Of course. What would be the point otherwise?"

Bailey blushed bright red. "You have to stop doing that!"

"Wanna see?"

"No!"

Olive grinned. "Yes, you do, but ya can't admit it. Maybe another day, darlin, maybe another day."

Bailey took a long breath. "Good night, Olive. See you in the morning."

"Sure will. I hope you're makin waffles, 'cause I want some."

Bailey woke up the next morning, spent a few minutes in the abbreviated gym in the garage, then went back inside for a shower. Jane - or maybe Olive - had sprung for some nice towels, so it was a luxurious experience.

She hit the kitchen, looking forward to making the promised waffles and a few strips of bacon. Olive was already sitting at the table, a hungry look in her eye. Bailey noted that Olive had her own little powdered sugar container, butter and syrup. Along with an empty plate and utensils.

Bailey grinned, poured batter, and then started the process. She made a waffle and tossed it on her plate, adding copious amounts of butter, then syrup. Looking back, Olive's plate had a waffle on it, the twin to Bailey's except more butter and some kind of maybe - jam? Bailey started another waffle, then sat to eat her own.

"What is that stuff on your waffle, Olive?"

"Fresh blackberry jam. Mmm ... don't you wish you could have some?"

"Nah, not really. I don't like the seeds."

"My blackberry jam doesn't have seeds, sugar."

"Sacrilege!"

"No, just no seeds."

"Oh. Ok. That's fine then."

They both grinned like madwomen and chomped on their waffles. Bailey had a second one and Olive mirrored it. Then, Olive had bacon on her plate and Bailey sat back, disappointed.

"I can't believe I forgot the bacon."

Olive shrugged, which was eye catching, considering the tight shirt and shorts she was wearing today. "Just toss some in the microwave for a couple minutes. It comes out pretty good."

"Oh, that's a good idea."

She grabbed the bacon package and threw four slices in the microwave, then tapped her foot impatiently while the bacon cooked. When the timer dinged, she grabbed at the bacon, burned herself on the steam and dropped it on the counter. "Ow."

"You need cookin' lessons, darlin. Maybe get that Dale man t' help."

"Psh. I cook just fine. You liked the waffles, didn't you?"

"I have to admit you did good on th' waffles."

Bailey smiled complacently. "Thanks. Next time you should try them with syrup."

"Sounds like a plan. You gonna wake up next to me next time?"

Bailey stuck out her tongue at Olive. "Not in THIS lifetime."

Olive made with a slow smile. "I got plenty of time. I'll check back next lifetime, then."

Bailey changed the subject. "Ok, so today we need to hunt down Laney. She's probably at her dad's house. Jane told her we would be there today, so at least she knows we're coming."

"Hey, how about our gambling trip?"

"I wouldn't miss it. But we'll wait till later, business first, missy."

Olive made some uncomplimentary sounds under her breath and Bailey chose to ignore it. Sometimes Olive acted more like a young child than the 25-year-old she appeared to be. Bailey figured it was natural for someone just adjusting to being a ... being.

Out in the garage, they piled into the Z3 and took off along Anime Street. Bailey still had to laugh at the name. Summerlin is about 25 miles from Henderson, and it was all freeway driving, so Bailey had a chance to open up her new toy a little. Speed limits are high in Nevada and it was fun to whip along the highway at 80mph.

20 miles goes by fast at 80mph though, and soon they pulled off into neighborhoods, making their way to the address on Sonatina Drive. Shortly after, they pulled up in front of a pretty house, with obligatory Spanish tile roofing, and stone and brick accents. It was painted in soft desert colors, with a pop of personality in the bright yellow door. The personality didn't stop at the door, either.

Bailey rang the bell, they waited awhile, then Bailey rang it again. They could hear it clearly inside, but no one came. Puzzled, they started to leave, but turned back for one more punch on the doorbell. Finally, sound of movement inside and the door opened on a stunning young woman dressed in a skimpy coverup, her long amber hair dripping.

"Hi, you must be from Washington? Daddy said you'd be by."

With that, she turned and set off toward the back of the house. With no invitation, the pair on the steps trailed along behind her, not sure if they'd been invited or not.

Bailey turned to Olive, "My, what a warm welcome. She's going to be stellar on the front desk job." Olive nodded grimly, for once the two of them being in perfect accord.

Out the back sliders they followed the girl, who dropped her coverup and made a perfect ten of a dive, then proceeded to do laps across the long end of the pool.

After a bit of standing awkwardly, Bailey and Olive stepped over to pool chairs and sat, silently waiting for Laney to finish her entrance. Or whatever it was she was doing.

Finally, she finished her laps apparently and surfaced near the ladder. She said to Bailey, "Sweetie, could you get me a towel?"

Bailey, already in a slow burn, grabbed a towel and tossed it to her.

Laney paraded around the pool apron, drying off and getting her hair up in the towel, then sitting at the table where the other two were. She lit up a cigarette and looked at them.

"Well, daddy said you'd probably wanting to make a job offer, but really, I'm planning on staying in the area and working this summer and I doubt you can match what I'll be making here. Sorry it was such a long trip for nothing." She shrugged helplessly, a 'what can you do' gesture.

Bailey paused a beat, then said, "Oh, I completely understand. Washington is quite some distance away and I'm sure that you'll be making more at your new job than the year's tuition and books that Jane was offering." She stood, followed by Olive, and they both started off toward the still open slider door. They made it almost to the door, when the voice came behind them, sounding a little strangled.

"Y-you're offering a year's tuition AND books for a couple months work?"

Bailey replied, "Oh no, darlin, that's what Jane WAS offering. Obviously, you have better things to do. And better places to do them."

With that, they both marched through the door, slid it carefully closed and then walked through the house, opening and closing the front door firmly. They had just made it to the car when the door flew open and Laney, with her towel hanging down in a disheveled mess, dashed out the door.

"Hey, uh, wait a minute! I'm sorry, I didn't understand - I was busy with ... um."

Bailey turned toward her, the fire showing in her eyes. "What did you want to say? I thought everything had already been said. Eloquently."

Laney had the grace to blush. "I'm sorry. I really am not usually this rude. I was reacting to my dad calling and telling me he'd found a job for me. He's got a habit of trying to control my life and I was ..." She ended it there.

"You were being a rude little career-ending bitch to get back at him? Is that what I'm hearing?"

Laney puffed up like she was going to explode, then stood down her DEFCON level, looked at her feet and said, "Yes, ma'am. I guess I was."

Bailey glared at her. She said, evenly, "If you weren't Dale's daughter, I'd be leaving you here in the dust. The offer for the books is withdrawn and you pay your own flight. If you're in Chelan five days from this minute, you'll have a job for the summer. In return, at the end of the job, UNLV will be paid directly by Jane's accountant for a year's tuition. And I'll be starting you with a toothbrush in the bathroom." Without another word, she turned on her heel, got in the car and started the engine. Olive barely managed to get in the car before it was flipping a U-turn and screaming back up the road they'd come in.

Olive's eyes were the size of dinner plates and she didn't say a word all the way back to Jane's house.

CHAPTER ELEVEN

May the Odds Be Ever In Your Favor.

When they got back to Jane's house, Bailey winked at Olive. "Did you like the show?"

"Show? Whatta ya mean?"

"With Laney - the blowup and threats and stuff?"

"That was a show? An act??"

"Of course. You don't think I'd really lose it over a silly job interview, do you?"

"Um. I never really thought about it."

"Well, trust me, you never lose your cool, especially with your employees. But now Laney thinks I'm a loose cannon and will tread gently."

Olive sighed. "I'm never gonna understand humans."

Bailey changed into a tight grey silk tee shirt and black jeans; and made ready to go to the casino. Olive made a statement with a black tee shirt and fashionably ripped jeans along with glaringly red shoes, and they called for a limo to pick them up.

While waiting for the car to arrive, Bailey said, "I have a confession, Olive. It wasn't all act. I shouldn't have let the little brat get to me in the first place - I've been breaking girls like her for years. It was just unexpected, since I was making the assumption that Dale's daughter would be as nice as him. Apparently, Jane's initial assessment of the wife was more accurate than we knew, since it seems that Laney has had someone else to use for a role model than Dale. I'm trying to give her the benefit of the doubt, but even with the ameliorating circumstances of her mother dying, I'm having a hard time excusing that much angst."

"Uh huh. I thought she was a bitch too. Um, Bailey ... "

A breath. "Yes, Olive?"

"Do I ever come off sounding like that?"

Bailey laughed. "Well, no, but you are a bit trying at times."

"Oh. I thought I was just being funny and edgy."

Gently, "Too much evening sitcom watching, dear. It's bad for you. Real people don't really live on nasty one-liners their whole lives."

"Time for me to grow up?"

"Oh, Olive. Never grow up. Just learn more when it's time to be edgy and when being edgy is just being a jackass."

Olive nodded, appearing to be actually listening. The doorbell rang and the driver was there with the car. They picked up their oh-so-tiny purses and split up. Bailey made her way to the long black Cadillac limo, and she was on her way. Olive cheated and simply vanished. Why walk anywhere when the teleport was available?

The driver pointed out the sights along the way once the car entered the Las Vegas Strip area, and finally deposited her in front of the Bellagio, its fountain in full glory with a medley of show tunes for the background music. Bailey had been to Vegas before on various junkets associated with being part of the publishing scene, but had never been in the Bellagio. Vegas seldom fails to amaze. She walked through the main concourse and down the hallways to the casino, where she stopped at the players club to sign up for a card. As long as she was going to spend money, she might as well get some free stuff for it. Her new card in hand, she walked along the various machines, starting easy with a $5 machine. The black card worked fabulously, and it wasn't long before she'd gotten lost in the daze of losing money just slightly faster than she won money.

Meanwhile, Olive had lifted off from the garage area of the house and angled her flight toward the Strip. She was still fascinated by the whole concept of the place. Sure losers all, they flocked to the Strip and begged to be fleeced of their rent money. She landed someplace inconspicuous between the Bellagio Hotel, and the casino. She figured it was about as close as she could get without someone noticing the air was very hard in this location.

She walked wide-eyed through the doors and up the long stone ramp to the main casino floor. It was a little difficult to walk among the people and keep from touching them or being touched by them - people may be unobservant, but running into a pretty girl and having her NOT be there would be disconcerting and might cause some kind of panic. She gave up and took on the wisp form, and flew the rest of the way to the casino area as a small ball of light, almost invisible among all the other balls of light in the Bellagio. Arriving inside, she looked around, lost in the overwhelming feelings of the people she was surrounded by. She had to turn on dampers for her sensors to keep from being overwhelmed. This made it harder to zoom in on Bailey, but she finally found her. She was playing slots and, of course, losing. But in such small amounts that Bailey could almost fool herself into thinking she was winning.

Olive came up alongside Bailey and whispered in her ear, "Spread it around a little, don't just stick to one machine. And make it look like you're just wandering, looking."

Bailey jumped and nearly dropped her drink, which sloshed over the edge and down her hand. "Hey, warn me next time!"

"I did warn you, I whispered in your ear."

"That's not warning, that's whispering in my ear."

"Stop already, people gonna think you crazy, talking to yourself like that."

Bailey shrugged and went back to the machine. "I'm doing really well, I won a $5000 jackpot!"

"Yeah, but you spent $6000 winning it."

"That's beside the point."

"We can't win at slots, it's too hard to influence the computer. So, play across the way until you stumble on the roulette wheel. Then, be fascinated by it."

"I AM fascinated by roulette. I have a system, I can win!"

"Uh huh. I bet. Ok, then you just hustle on over there, slowly, and win."

Bailey pulled her money out of the machine and tried another one, a $10 machine this time. She managed to win another $5k jackpot, only spending 9k to get it. Another machine brought her amazingly close to being back to breaking even, she still had nearly 90k of her limit. She was laughing internally about considering only being down ten thousand dollars to be "breaking even" and began to get a better feel for those people who did this kind of thing all the time.

She wandered closer to the roulette wheels, and finally stepped up to one of them and asked for some chips. She'd done a bit of roulette playing before, but nothing more than two or three hundred dollars at most. She took a breath and asked for $1000 in chips. She immediately put $200 on 22 black, and lost. Quickly. Mustering her thoughts, she started using her foolproof "system" and lost the entire $1000 in a few minutes. Annoyed, and knowing it was only a matter of getting the right rhythm, she bought another $5000 in chips. It took a few more minutes this time, but she lost all that as well. She frowned; a bit discouraged.

Then the voice in her head said, "Ready to try it my way?"

Afraid to nod much, Bailey thought, "Ok, I guess."

"Buy 10k and let's see what happens."

Bailey bought another 10k worth of chips, shocked at how fast that seemingly huge 100k had gone down. She chose 22 red, for variety, and put a thousand on it. She won. She smiled and let it ride. And again. And again. The table began to quiet, and people were staring. She let it ride again. And again. Finally, with complete silence around her, she held up her hands and pulled her winnings out. She smiled at the croupier, and left a stack of chips in front of him. One of the casino employees carried her winnings to the Redemption Center and helped her shove them through the window. She smiled at the girl and gave her several tokens, then waited for her cashout.

She'd won $1,430,000 after the tips. Of course, taxes still had to come out, and she spent a lengthy time in the casino offices, verifying her win. In fact, she was there all night and well into the morning. Since she was deep in the bowels of the casino by the time she got to that point, she didn't even have any moral support from Olive, she was on her own. She noticed they were polite in the extreme, someone kept bringing her drinks or bits of food. Some perfectly cooked prime rib served by a chef in a white hat. A nice jacket with the MGM lion on it. But one thing she noticed, there was never any thought that she might leave. She was sure they were going over every inch of film they had on her, trying to find some reason to disqualify her wins. But in the end, they congratulated her, even gave her one of those giant checks and took her picture with it.

They were also offered all kinds of comps, and she had a great few days on the town, limo rides anywhere she wanted, and tours of all the MGM properties. Drinks with famous people and a blur of fashion and food. Sadly, Olive wasn't able to join her on most of her tours, she "stayed in their room" and "ate room service." However, Bailey did not spend one thin dime of her winnings at the gaming tables, and while many low-level employees got extremely generous tips, Bailey had learned her lesson about gaming. The house never loses. At least without help.

Finally, when the end of the fairy tale arrived, she bundled herself back on the plane and flew out of McCarran with a light heart. Of course, having a big bunch more money in her retirement account helped with that a bit.

CHAPTER TWELVE

Meanwhile, back at the ranch.

I have to admit that with the house empty of people, it was kind of
lonely. I'd gotten used to Bailey and Olive being around, and before
that Kit had been my constant companion. And Dale, as well. Today
though, it was just me and Jandice. So, I sat on the couch and petted the cat,
and wandered outside and sat in the perfect mid-afternoon sunshine,
listening to the faint sounds of the people at play down by the lake, and the
distant noises from the waterpark down the way.

My thoughts turned to Cai Shun and what he might be wanting to see me
about. I assumed it had to be something to do with Kit and the part of the
ship that Mister Shun had been such an instrumental part of acquiring. He'd
always seemed to be interested in me, and thinking about it, it was possible
that he'd known far more about me than he'd ever let on. I suppose that he'd
had plenty of time to run as many checks on me as he wanted to, what with
me sending him a letter of introduction and asking questions. As soon as he
or his staff had seen "Jane Bond" on the letterhead, they must have been full
of questions. I could see them in my mind's eye looking at Facebook pictures

of me and poring over questions and answers I'd given to various and sundry sources over the years. Once something is on the internet, it's always there. The only thing you can hope for is to live a life of obscurity and hope no one ever noticed you. Obviously, having a prophecy about you (or at least someone who looks like you and has your name) would make you a person of interest.

Still, I suppose there's very little I can do except wait here and see what he writes back - and what he says when he arrives. Who knows, he might just want to pick up some apples at the source.

As Olive might say, "Yeah, right."

It is a little hard to believe. You don't fly thousands of miles for some apples you could order on Amazon - or send a minion to pick up. I'll have to make sure to take him down to Cashmere to visit the orchard owned by a friend. She and her husband have been together making apples for most of the last 20 years, and the orchard has been in the family for generations. The apples won't be ready to eat, but they'll definitely be big enough to see on the trees. She says they're changing over to pears, which is inconvenient since I don't like pears as much as apples. That didn't seem to make a dent in her wishes though, she said something about making more money. No one thinks about MY needs.

I guess I'll just put it out of my head and forget it, for now.

I did find myself wondering how Bailey and Olive were getting along on their trip to Las Vegas. I hoped they wouldn't find it all too boring. I'd planned it as best I could to let them do as little as possible in terms of having silly errands. After all, they were basically on a silly errand for me, might as well make it painless.

Next morning, or it was nearly noon actually, Bailey sent me a text letting me know that she and Olive would be staying in Vegas a week or so. Apparently, Bailey had won a substantial amount of money and they wanted to look around Vegas while they were there. Since I'd bought the house there for that very reason, I thought it was an excellent idea. Plus, after the initial loneliness, I was rather liking the feeling of having my house to myself again. She did send a rather cryptic text though, too. "The bitch arrives in three days." I sent her back a reply saying "I thought you weren't coming home for a week" but, apparently she didn't think it was funny enough to warrant a comeback. At any rate, I didn't hear from either of them that week.

I was lying in the front yard on my most comfortable lounger, in my teeniest red bikini, when I heard a car in the driveway. I lay there for a bit, ignoring it, assuming it was the mail. However, pretty soon I heard the ding of the front doorbell. I hopped up and scampered over to grab my coverup - it really is a TEENY bikini - and went to answer the door.

Laney was at the door! She had a slightly trepidatious look on her face, but forged ahead anyhow.

"Good morning, Jane. How are you today?

"I'm wonderful, Laney!" I gave her a big hug, which after some hesitation she returned.

"Is Bailey here?"

"Nope, no Bailey, no Olive. I'm here alone basking in the sun, as you can see from my less than businesslike attire."

Oddly, she seemed to relax a little and said, "Oh, well, that's fine. I have things to bring in, am I staying here or in a hotel?"

"Actually, neither, honey. You'll be staying at Bailey's house. We decided since you'd be working with her quite a lot, and she spends so much time here it would be a natural for you to room with her! She's very fun, I'm sure you'll have a great time."

She replied faintly, "Thank you, yes, I'm sure I'll have fun."

"Let me get some clothes on and I'll take you over to her house so you can get unpacked. Bailey won't be home for a couple days, so you can get the lay of the land and maybe spend a day on the beach."

"Thank you, that would be fine, Jane."

"Come on in, have a seat in the kitchen, and I'll be right back."

I galloped down the hallway and grabbed some clothes and jumped into them. I was looking forward to spending some time with Laney and this seemed like the perfect opportunity to get to know her, just the two of us.

I went back out to the kitchen, Laney was sitting, looking out the window. She seemed enthralled by the view.

When she saw me, she remarked, "I don't see a lot of grass and trees back home. Most people don't have those, since water is so expensive. Using it to keep a patch of decorative lawn alive is really not worth it in most cases."

"Yup, I can definitely see that. We're pretty much in the middle of the desert here as well, but with a lake of our own we have enough water to waste on luxuries, I guess."

She said quickly, "Oh, I don't mean it's a waste, I just mean it's not worth half your month's salary to have a lawn. I love having a little patch of grass. Daddy's always been willing to pay some extra to keep a little speck of lawn at our house, and I'm grateful for it, when I see most people's front yards made of bits of scraggly grass and weeds."

I nodded. "Coffee? Tea?" With a smile, I added, "I have Pepsi Max as well."

She grinned. "Daddy's gotten to you, I see. That's a good sign." She eyed me speculatively. "So, what do you see in him?"

"Rich old man, nice house, decent money ... "

She gaped at me, then shut her mouth nearly with a snap and nodded. "Sense of humor too, I see."

"I like to think so." I put my hand out to shake, "Jane Bond"

"Laney McDaniel. Nice to meet you, Ms. Bond."

"Likewise, Ms. McDaniel."

"So, was it Max, tea, coffee? Or ... I suppose we have water if you're one of those people. I guess we have water, anyhow. Did you know that our water here in Chelan is so pure they have to put additives in it to bring it down to standards? At least that's the urban legend I heard, and I like it, so I'm making sure it gets passed on."

Laney sat and looked at me for a bit. "I can see why he likes you. You're not what I expected, for some reason."

I shrugged. "Well, I'm not ever sure what people expect, so I just plan on being me. Who do you plan on being, Laney?"

She seemed taken aback by the question. "I don't know. I guess I'm still making plans."

I nodded. "That's an excellent answer." I leaned in. "But you never did tell me if you wanted something to drink."

She broke into laughter. "I'll take the Max, it starts to grow on you. And if I asked for Coke, I figure that daddy would have a coronary - even from this distance."

I pulled a cold Max out of the fridge, got a glass and some ice and gave it all to her. I figured she had to do some of it on her own.

"So, what are you expecting to do here, Laney? How much did Bailey tell you?"

Oddly enough, she blushed a little. "I ... um."

"Didn't Bailey go through the job description, expectations and salary with you?"

Finally, in a rush of words, she said, "I pissed Bailey off and she walked off without saying anything but that if I got here in five days on my own, I had a job. It was my fault, I was being a bitch. She even told me I was being a bitch."

I sat and looked at her a bit. "It's pretty tough, isn't it? Having to be cold and hard, when you really just want to curl up and die. And then when the only other person you truly care about runs away and leaves you alone. But you can't let him know how much you're hurting." I put my hand on her hand across the table. "I'm sorry, Laney."

For just a moment she was vulnerable, but then the stone walls went up and the steel gates came down and she was cold and tough again.

"Sometimes you just have to be a bitch, Jane. And sometimes you know when to bow down to the inevitable, and a full year's tuition is enough to put up with anything."

I looked into her eyes, but found only coldness there. I nodded. "Fair enough. We'll be opening a detective agency. Bailey and I don't know much about computers, especially about what goes on behind the scenes. That's what we want you to assemble for us - a computer system that can be taken care of by general contractors, once we have you put it all together. It will likely require you to work long days and long nights, but I think we've paid in advance enough to assure your willingness. Your budget will be essentially unlimited, but Olive has a talent for discovering creative bookkeeping. And never ever lie to her. She will know. Trust me. Other than that, I'd prefer anything you bought to be locally sourced, but I'm fully aware of the impossibility of that. After all, we went to a location in New York for our conference equipment." With that, I handed her one of the carbon cards and went to get Threepio to carry her luggage to Bailey's house. Over the next few days, I saw her carting things in and out. I saw her leave in Threepio very early one morning and come back late that evening, stuffed to the gills with boxes bearing names like HP, Dell and IBM. And things started to come together, at least as far as I could tell. I mean, it looked very techy, and in the end, I trusted her.

I received a reply from Cai Shun in my email. He's as charming in email as he is in person, and he says he's looking forward to meeting with me and I should consider where we should go to showcase the area. And the apples. He seems a bit obsessed with apples, if you ask me, but maybe they don't have them there like we do here. I'm putting together a list of places to go, and I thought I'd visit a few in the next few days. I offered a seat to Laney, thinking she might want to go with me and get acquainted with the area, but muttering something about Bailey, she said that she'd rather just work on the computers. Bailey must have really made an impression on her!

I'm going to take Mister Shun to Karma Vineyards - it's one of my favorite places and the view is just amazing. Another one I want to make sure of visiting is Fielding Hills Winery. They have a seating area that looks out over the entire valley and it's another amazing view. If we get a chance, we might go take a look at Cave B Winery. It's near the Gorge Amphitheatre in George, Washington. It's another one with stunning views. I'm not much of a wine drinker, but love the food and views!

The little town of Cashmere is chock full of apple orchards, and I happen to know a small orchardist. I'll get her and her husband to take us around their place. As I mentioned, it's too early in the year for there to be much in the way of real apples, but seeing the little apples making their way into the world is a pretty cool thing as well.

Bailey and Olive came back at the end of the week, and after a terse confrontation with Laney in the first few minutes, I guess they all settled who the big dog was, and everyone was comfortable with that. The computer systems continue to grow, but really all I see when I look in there (behind the closed, locked door) is black racks with black computer faces and lots of twinkly lights. I figured out why they call them racks, too. It's torture just standing in front of them, especially in the cold wind that the air conditioning makes. I shiver just looking at it, but Olive seems as thrilled as Laney. Of course, some of it with Olive is a near giggle-fit when she looks at the "beyond antique" equipment. I ignore her.

The days fly by, and I find time to sneak off to the beach with Bailey a few times, lying in the sun pretending we don't have a care in the world. The nice thing is, at this juncture we really don't.

At some point though, all good things must come to an end, and next week Cai Shun will be here and finally I'll get to find out what exactly it is that he wants. Because I know he wants something. And I'm also not sure why I'm finding dread in his coming here. Perhaps it's just the unknown. Perhaps it's fear of having to make a decision on whether to tell him about Olive and the rest of Kit's story. Because, like it or not, that's why he's really on the way. No matter what bit of information, what olive branch of hope he'll offer, he'll be expecting to get something from this trip, especially since he never really got even his curiosity assuaged last time.

And unfortunately, I know I owe him.

He's arriving on Amtrak in Wenatchee. I plan to meet him and drag him home to Chelan with me. I've banished Bailey and Lacey to Bailey's house so I can have him to myself. Likely I'll slave over breakfast the next morning (I hope he likes omelettes since it's the only thing I can cook reliably) but we'll eat someplace in Wenatchee that night, since the train arrives from Seattle between 8:30 and 9:00pm. I hope he doesn't have too much of a retinue, as even taking Threepio we'll only have enough seats for six or seven people. If there are a number of people with him, we'll probably drop them off at the Marriot and let them fend for themselves. I do get a chance to giggle a bit at thinking of Bailey's idea of Burger King. But, in the clear light of day, it actually might not be that bad an idea. Of course, I'd be thinking more of EZ's Burgers than Burger King.

Of course, all this may go by the wayside if he has a limo waiting, an itinerary lined up with a list of places to visit, and a hotel all picked out.

Tomorrow night. I'll know tomorrow night, and I'm on pins and needles even if it all turns out to be my imagination and he really is just here for some apples.

Friday morning dawned perfectly, with blue sky and the promise of hot but not blistering heat. The train doesn't get in until around 9pm but I decided to head to Wenatchee early and do some yard saling. Yard saling is an interesting psychological concept. On the one hand, you're looking for junk - looking through other people's junk and picking and choosing what of their junk you want to make your junk. But over and above that, it's a chance to sneak in and judge them on their taste, get a good look at the inside of their garage, critique their landscape choices and of course, see if they're doing a better job of upkeep on their house and grounds than you. Plus, the added bonus of seeing someone else growing exactly that kind of plant you know would look attractive in your yard. Or, alternatively, seeing that what you'd intended to buy would be hideous in five years. In other words, completely legal and above board spying on the neighbors. I love it! I spent a couple hours, got a couple books and a couple silly things that I thought Bailey and Olive would enjoy. I did manage to find an old Dilbert book for Laney, but I have despaired of finding anything to crack that frozen exterior. That first day when I saw a glimmer of humanity in her has never returned, and she's frozen even harder.

Later in the afternoon I picked up some snacks at WalMart and went down to the Amtrak depot. I love trains of all kinds and so had a nice afternoon sitting in my little foldup chair, reading my book, eating my snacks and watching trains go by. Wenatchee has the distinction of being one of the funnels that most of the train traffic in Washington State goes through, so it's a great place to watch trains. Bulk oil trains, long container cars filled with Chinese stock for Christmas or next summer for all I know. Train cars full of automobiles, and I really had the luck this time, as I saw a couple of shiny green Boeing 737 airplane fuselages going through. I guess they make them back east somewhere and ship them up to Everett for final assembly.

And I got more nervous as the day went by. Finally, 8:30 came and my Amtrak app told me that the train was on time, so it should be here at about 8:50. I stood and looked down the tracks and I could see the big single light as it rounded the corner, coming toward me, coming right at me, sailing past me - as the brakes came on and the engineer did a perfect stop with the passenger cars for this area right at the platform. The attendants put the little yellow metal step out and people began to file out. Most of them just for a smoke break, but Wenatchee has a decent train travel interest and there were quite a few getting on and getting off.

And then I saw him, his distinguished head standing out from the rest. He was coming down the steps and out the door, then looking around to see if anyone was there to greet him. I'd expected him to have at least an assistant or two, but oddly enough, he was completely alone.

When he saw me, he grinned. "I was expecting a large black limousine with a neat trim driver and sign with my name spelled incorrectly on it. Instead I have Jane Bond, in person."

I smiled back at him and said, "Well, I figured you might be sick of royal treatment by now, so you just got me, instead."

To my surprise, he came over and hugged me. "It is well to see you, my friend. I am happy we've met again."

After my initial shock, I hugged him back. He's a very huggable person.

"I was rather hoping to meet the estimable Threepio, and it seems that might be the case, lacking the long black limousine."

"You are amazingly astute, mister Shun. My friend Bailey told me you might be tired of unctuous politicians and I should pick you up in person and take you to Burger King. She was kidding about Burger King, but seeing you here looking so human, how would you feel about a genuine American burger?"

"It would be a pleasure, Miss Bond. I can't think of anything I'd rather have at this moment. For the most part, state dinners serve you the same sort of food that you eat when you're at home. Everyone seems to forget that perhaps you've tired of everyday fare."

I smiled. "Sounds like a plan, Threepio's sitting in the parking lot, and EZ's Burgers is on the way home. I had made the assumption you'd be staying with me in Chelan. I hope that wasn't presumptuous?"

"Actually, Miss Bond, I'd hoped to try the American custom of 'couch surfing', if I have the term correct?"

I actually laughed out loud. "Mister Shun, you are so much different than I was expecting. But I hate to disappoint you, I have the guest room all made up and ready for you. Couch surfing won't be necessary!"

The nice thing about living in small towns is that airports, bus lounges and train depots are correspondingly small. Threepio was parked about 15 feet from where Mister Shun debarked from his train, so it was a short walk. We tossed in Cai's surprisingly small amount of luggage and closed the van's barn door. We both got buckled in and I cranked up Threepio and we backed out of the lot, turned and made our way to the main street and headed out of town.

We stopped in at EZ's and got two magnificent Tillamook Cheese and Bacon burgers and sat in their parking lot, dripping into our napkins. I became Jane, and he became Cai and by the time the huge burgers were gone, we had established a friendship. We sat and watched the remains of the sunset and headed to Chelan in the dark, chatting on the way.

"Are you really here for the apples, Cai?"

"Oh, absolutely! I have a passion for apples. I'll make sure I have some Red Delicious apples, they are such an American tradition." I could hear the twinkle in his eye. "Of course, I like the wines too, and I expect you're planning on taking me to visit some of the local cellars."

"You can't really visit Washington Wine Country without having wine, now can you? It wasn't that many years ago that grapes in Washington were practically unheard of, and now you see them on every rocky, sandy knoll. It's perfect weather and soil for grapes - who knew?"

"Apparently someone knew - and took advantage of it."

I nodded, for all the good it did in the darkened van. "Yes, that's certain. And I'm sure it's an interesting story."

We rode on in companionable silence, discussing bits of ideas. He mentioned how much nicer the Amtrak ride was than our memories of the Beijing to Lhasa train trips. We both agreed on that.

110

Driving past the dark and silent lake, we took the turn and made our way up into the hills where my house lies. We pulled in the barn and made our way down the path to the house. I'd made sure to ask Olive about checking on the lights between the barn and the house, and as per usual she'd outdone herself and the path was perfect, bathed in a soft yellowish glow that came from the lamps spaced along the way. I was sure that the path would never have snow on it, and that dirt would somehow magically disappear. But I tried not to think about that and hoped my mother wasn't watching that sort of thing that closely. I wouldn't put it past her, though.

We arrived at the house. Alexa (or perhaps Olive) greeted us with the same warm glow in the house as we came inside. I kicked on the main lights in the kitchen area, my favorite part of the house. Cai apparently agreed, as he looked around the room appreciatively.

"Stainless Steel is certainly the most desired kitchen appliance finish, isn't it? Do you suppose that in twenty-five years Americans reality show hosts will be looking at the hopelessly dated steel fixtures and black granite counters and muttering to their television audience 'what were they thinking', or do some things transcend time?"

I stared at my beautiful kitchen and said, "Well, I'm not sure about that, truthfully. But I'd bet that the people who put in the avocado oven and fridge with the white Formica tile counter thought they were the epitome of fashion in the 60's. And I can't see that not being the same idea in 20 years. After all, the vicious circle has to continue - the snake has to eat his tail to keep the whole carousel in motion, right?" I smiled. "Pink and black appliances and counters were all the rage in the 1950's, maybe that will come back in 2040."

Cai shuddered. "Perhaps. However, I do not expect to be here to see it."

We shuffled back outside to gather luggage and after rolling it down the path, delivered it to Cai's room. I pointed out the bathroom, towels and other appurtenances and then, yawning even though it was fairly early, I bid him good night and slid into my own bed. I did not so much as dream the rest of the night, or if I did, they were stealthy dreams that stayed inside my head.

I woke early, but it sounded like there were people out in the kitchen area. I stumbled out there in my uncaffeinated state and looked around, a little befuddled. Olive was sitting munching on some kind of breakfast burrito, Bailey had a sausage bacon biscuit of some kind and Cai was chowing down on pancakes with syrup - and a sausage patty on the side. Laney was scarfing scrambled eggs. I looked in the bag and grabbed an egg muffin, it seemed the most logical. I also started the Keurig to making me some wake-up juice.

"What is this? Time to scare Jane out of her mind? All these people around!"

Somewhat indistinctly though her biscuit, Bailey said, "I have no idea, they just followed me here. We were just all ..." Here she paused to swallow, "hungry and thought we'd like to meet Cai, so, here we are."

She stage-whispered to me, "He's cute!"

Cai laughed. "Thank you, Miss Bailey. At my age we take all the disingenuous comments we can. We don't get any others."

She smirked. "It was actually the truth, but you won't believe that."

"Sad fact of life, is it not?"

"What, that we never believe good things about ourselves?"

"Yes, Miss Bailey, we never do. We believe the bad things in a heartbeat, but the good things never really reach inside."

We all sighed at the wisdom of this statement, and silently munched our various breakfast items.

After a bit, Cai said, "I seem to have put a damper on this conversation. I beg your pardon for being the ... er ... wet blanket, I believe is the term."

I waved my hands around in the air, saying, "No, it's just morning. Morning is rough for most of us, in fact I think Laney is the only one of us that really seems to like it in the morning."

Laney shrugged, her eyes on Olive. She seemed fascinated by Olive's eating of her breakfast. It made we wonder if I'd better talk with Olive about keeping her nature more under wraps. Olive looked perfectly normal, but anytime she was in a social gathering there was also the stress of making sure she didn't wind up interacting with anyone that would expect her to actually exist.

Laney remarked, "I love how morning smells - how all the heat from the day before bakes the earth, and overnight it renews, the dews come down and it just activates all that perfume normally locked inside a plant. Morning on the desert is the best thing in the world."

I must admit I was taken aback a bit by Laney's most poetic viewpoint. "I agree, in fact, I'd much rather be up early during the summer - you feel like you're missing so much otherwise. In the winter, I could really not care less. In fact, what I'd most care about is staying in bed and considering my options for breakfast."

As we chomped through our repast, we discussed weather, time, tennis and world peace. We didn't get far in solving any problems but admitting there is a problem might be the best beginning to a solution.

"Bailey, can I borrow your car?"

"Sure, I'm sticking around here today anyhow. Laney is putting the finishing touches on some of the computer stuff and I want to watch it all come up. I'll also be checking some of the software - so knock yourself out. And of course, we have Threepio if we need a car."

"Thanks, sweetie. I thought Cai might like an opportunity to see the area and your car is perfect for that."

"My car is perfect for everything. Except maybe hauling large bags of mulch back from WalMart. Threepio is perfect for that."

"I should consider a Jeep. I've always wanted a Jeep."

"Why not another BMW?"

I considered a moment, then, "I love your Z3, but I've always wanted a Jeep, from very early. I think it's because it has all the things your Z has, but the Jeep has four-wheel drive.

"Good point. My BMW tends to like the mud a lot less than even Threepio."

"Anyhow, I thought we'd head over to Fielding Hills, maybe do a little tasting, then probably do lunch at Karma. I'll have to leave the tasting to Cai though, since I'll be driving!"

Bailey wiggled her eyebrows at me. I rolled my eyes at her. So eloquent.

Since it was a Saturday morning, I decided we'd go visit some yard sales. Early bird and the worm and all that. I've never been partial to worms, but it's certainly a reality when visiting yard sales!

There are few if any yard sales in China, so Cai was unfamiliar with the browsing through other people's crap at their houses. I figured it was also a great way to introduce him to our culture, so called at least. So, to that end, we spent the next couple hours driving around in Bailey's little car, gathering a few very small treasures for him to take back with him. For my part, I found a very odd little evil looking duck - like a rubber ducky, but with a scowl and fangs. I thought it was hilarious, having an evil rubber ducky.

The wine cellars and tours start to come to life late morning, usually almost noon. We tasted wine at a couple places, had lunch at Karma - always a treat - and then wandered around the area finding small out of the way places. Finally, we wound our way down to the lake, where we sat and watched people for an hour or so. I was astounded how much in stride Cai took all of this, although I don't know why. So much of what I know about China and Tibet comes from bits of inaccurate information gathered online or in sitcoms. Why should I expect that to come anywhere close to reality when everything you see on TV is so far from it? At any rate, Cai seemed to have fun and really enjoy himself. We finalized our day with a burger by the Lake, and while we were munching our fries, Cai asked what Olive was.

I paused with my mouth open, a fry hanging out, then came back to life a second later and managed to continue to eat, but suddenly the fry became tasteless and weird.

"What do you mean, Cai? Olive is ... Olive. Just a woman we have working here with us."

He chewed ruminatively on a fry and finally said, "No, she is not. I am not sure what she is, but it is not human. It is a very perfect simulation, but from the very first this morning, I could tell something was off. For instance, I know how many items of food there were in the bag, but even though Olive was eating one of them, nothing appeared to have been taken from the bag. I thought it might be my imagination. However, I saw her discard the wrapper in the trash, but there was nothing there when I looked a bit later. No, she is not real. She is amazing, but she is not real."

I admit my hackles rose a little at that, and I said, "She's every bit as real as you or I, Cai. She's amazing and we all love her. I'm not sure what you mean by her not being real, but I assure you it's not true."

He raised his hands in mock surrender and said, "I understand more than you might think. And yes, I see that she is a real person. But she is not inhabiting a real body. Is that more of an accurate representation of the facts?"

I hid behind the fries for a while, eating them with a lot more concentration than they really deserved. Finally, though, I had to say something. "Should we take dessert back with us?"

"I believe we should. What sort of dessert do your friends desire?"

"Generally speaking, things with alcohol in them."

"Perhaps we should find the makings for some sort of punch drink and take that with us, along with a few bottles of a variety of liquor?"

"I think that's an excellent idea. This seems like it would be a great night to get totally wasted."

He shrugged. "It was just an idle question - we can let it drop if you wish."

I sighed. "No, it will have to be answered, I suppose. In fact, I had the intention of talking with you about it later. After all, you were instrumental in ... well, more about that later."

"As you wish, Jane."

"Thank you, Cai."

We made a stop at Safeway and gathered the means for a feast, including my favorite snack foods and accessories. We also got a boatload, almost literally, of drinkables and mixers and managed to get it all in the Z3's tiny trunk. We hauled our booty home, and pulled up in the drive, still at least an hour before sunset. It sounded like the party had started already, music could be heard through the open doors, and I could hear voices at various volumes.

Cai and I gathered some of the food and took it inside, meeting Bailey at the door. I sent her out to grab the leftovers and bring them in. The remains of a pizza and from the looks of it, a very large sub sandwich, lay on the dining room table. Laney and Olive were standing with drinks in their hands, talking in low tones, and they reacted to our arrival with much joyful noise. They had apparently been sampling what we had already in stock, for Laney seemed more at ease than usual. In fact, she seemed to have thawed several degrees. As we stood there, Bailey came in the door with the rest of the goodies and we spread everything out in a smorgasbord display. Everyone began chatting and eating, but it didn't miss my notice how much of Cai's time was spent on watching Olive. Interesting that the same curiosity seemed to envelope Laney, as she was talking and laughing with Olive, but there was a distinct look of waiting for something. Or at least watching for something.

We worked our way through what was left of the sub sandwich and made a slew of alcoholic drinks - plenty of daiquiris and icy drinks, and even some drinks without any additives. I was sitting on the couch, looking off at the sunset when Laney sat down beside me. She looked a little sad.

"What's the matter, hon? Are you all right?"

She nodded. "I'm fine. Just a little tired."

"Mmhm. That's the line I use when I don't want to tell someone the truth."

"It's the truth!"

"Is it, sweetie?"

She sighed a long sigh. "No, of course not. I'll be leaving for Las Vegas soon, my time here is almost up."

"You'll miss Chelan that much? I thought you spent most of your time working on the computers - did you even get to the beach?"

She smiled. "No, I never got to the beach."

"Well, then, what's the deal? I kind of thought you were looking forward to being gone. After all, you're just here for the money, right?"

She looked sideways at me for a moment. "Yeah. I guess so."

"Uh huh. Sounds like "just a little tired" to me."

"I'll miss Olive."

"Huh?"

She gave a kind of sorry laugh. "I'll miss Olive. I've spent so much time with her over the past few weeks, getting computer equipment ready and setting things up. She's so smart and so much fun to be around. It's like I gained a best friend, but I'll never see her again."

I blinked. "Oh."

"Uh huh. She so vivacious, she's more alive than anyone I've ever met. She knows so many things, she can talk on so many levels. And I feel sorry for her."

"Sorry for her? Why??"

"Well, honestly, I'm not sure. But I know she has some sort of muscular disease."

I sputtered, "Muscular disease?"

"Yes. I'm sure it's something like that - she never picks anything up. I can tell she wants to, but she's just not able. Small things like papers or cups, that sort of thing seems to be fine, but anything of any weight, she's just not able to handle it. And she works so hard to hide it. It must be so frustrating to her."

"I ... well ... you ... seem to have it all figured out."

She nodded. "I'll come back, of course. Do you know what it is that causes it, Jane?"

"Yes. She's confided in me. And I can't tell you, but I will say that she's working on it and we're hoping someday she might be able to ... better manipulate the world than she can right now."

At that moment Olive came over. "Hey, what you two talkin about so serious-like over here?"

Laney looked at the floor. "I was just feeling sorry that I'll be leaving soon, and I've gotten used to you all, I'll miss you. All."

Olive nodded. "Aye, I bet. Well, I'm gonna miss you too, Laney." And then she reached over and smoothed Laney's hair, brushed her cheek with her hand and then bent and placed a kiss on her forehead. "It's not quite time to leave yet, we have quite a bit of polishing to do. So, let's concentrate on that and not worry too much about the future."

Olive strode off, moving back into the kitchen area and leaving all of us behind, spread out on the couch. I looked after her in disbelief, not able to understand what I'd just seen. Out of the corner of my eye, I could see Cai sitting back in his chair, completely nonplussed at what he'd just seen.

I swallowed. "She's pretty amazing, all right. I feel lucky to have her here."

Laney nodded. "I've never met anyone like her - so completely sunk in talk about computers and servers at one second and down rolling in the mud talking about boyfriends and sex the next."

I laughed. "Yeah, boyfriends and sex. She seems to know a lot about that, too."

"Mmhmm. She's certainly given me some food for thought about all that. And about everything, Jane. She's brilliant."

Laney got up, kissed ME on the forehead and headed back to the table where she grabbed the makings of another drink. She walked over to the couch where Cai was sitting and said "Dance, mister Shun?"

He smiled and said, "I thought you would never ask."

And with that, they got up and started doing an impromptu dance in the tiny area left by people and food. Bailey came over and collapsed on the couch next to me. She looked at the two of them dancing, then at me.

"What the hell, Jane? Hands? Lips?"

"I have no idea, Bailey. I've seen her cry, though."

"Well, there's definitely something going on."

"Just in time too - Cai was asking some pointed questions about her earlier today and I saw Laney gazing at her while we were eating. Little did I know that she's just found a BFF, maybe for the first time. Or maybe it's hero worship. At least it wasn't what I thought it was."

"Yea. I figured we'd have to talk to her about Olive sooner or later, but maybe not, now.

"Laney aside, what about Cai?"

"After that display, I don't think he's got as much to wonder about?"

"I guess. And we have more to wonder about."

"Yeah. Quite a lot."

The party went on for another hour or so. Cai Shun went to his room at that point and the rest of us kind of wound down together. Obviously, no one was driving home, so we split up among the various rooms. Laney and

Bailey wound up in the guest room, Olive opted for the couch, all cocooned in a blanket she brought out from somewhere. It was a warm night, and everyone was a bit more than a bit tipsy. Sleep came on almost immediately.

Later that night, I felt a presence and the small pink light that Olive had affected before she really began to wear her "body" all the time, tinkled at the door, then flickered in my room.

"Hello, Olive."

"Hi, Jane. I'm really sorry about that. I never intended for anything to go that far."

"Go ... how far, dear?"

"To get so connected to a human. Laney and I seem to just click and it's hard to keep that separation. I hope you're not too angry at me for the hands and the kiss."

I smiled at her. "No, not at all. In fact, it worked out perfect. I think you convinced Cai that you're a real person. And, of course, I think that Laney has about half fallen in love with you."

"Yeah. Half or more. It's kind of agonizing, Jane. I never expected ... "

"To quote a famous poet, life is what happens when you're making other plans."

"I thought that was John Lennon."

"You don't think John was a poet?"

"Oh. Well, yeah, I guess so. But you're distracting me. And I'm not making other plans. But it's still disquieting."

"Oh, Olive. Welcome to being human."

"Does it always hurt like this?"

"No, sometimes it's much worse."

"Oh, something to look forward to, eh?

"Uh huh."

Her voice grew diffident. "I'm in power save mode right now, recharging at my fullest extent. It took - well - enough energy to drain Lake Roosevelt, to manifest those hands.

"I saw your little twinkle and thought it might be something like that. How long before you're back to yourself again."

"Not long, really. I bounce back pretty fast. But I did want you to know it was a desperation ploy and that it's not something I'm able to do on a whim."

"It's all right, Olive. And for that matter, I think it's amazing. I hereby authorize you to expand your capacity with the idea of being able to manifest more fully."

"I - you're sure, Jane Bond? That's a lot of power."

"I have faith in you, Olive. I know you'll use your powers for good." I had to snicker at the last part, and she laughed with me.

"Now, can I go back to sleep?"

"Yes, you can now. And can you see me rolling my eyes at you?"

"I can now. Can you see me sticking my tongue out at you?"

"I can now. G'night, Jane."

"G'night, Olive."

CHAPTER THIRTEEN

"Fell off a wall"

Morning dawned as per usual. Only most of us had no idea what we might be facing. After the night we'd had, everyone had gone back to sleep, or at least had pretended to sleep.

Laney appeared to be back to her old surly self, although I think we were at least hung over to some extent. Myself, I had a nasty headache, and everything was too bright and clear. And loud. Olive had "gone to town early" according to a note left on the table. Cai Shun had yet to make his appearance. Bailey looked her usual perfect self, but I could see signs of wear about the eyes and corners of her mouth. She was hurting. Why DO we do these things to ourselves?

We all sat around the table, drank orange juice and ate Eggos. Nasty things, for the most part, but it was what there was, and I wasn't about to make omelettes, feeling the way I felt.

After a half hour or so, Cai Shun came into the kitchen looking way too chipper for his age and the amount I'd seen him drink last night. "Morning, ladies!"

"What are YOU so happy about?" This from Bailey.

"Me? Happy? Why do you ask?"

Laney snarled, "Because you said, 'morning, ladies' and that's enough for a hanging right there."

He looked at the two of them. "My goodness, looks like someone has gotten up on the wrong side of the bed."

I smirked. "Yeah, or wrong side of the floor. "

They both grumped at me. I suggested to Cai that we head out for breakfast. An hour of seeing other people in misery had greatly improved my hangover. He agreed, and we headed out to where the cars are, then up to the barn when we realized Olive had taken the smartcar and I hadn't stolen Bailey's keys again.

"I think I need to buy a Jeep."

"Why? I thought you were in love with your van?"

"Oh, I am. But sometimes it's just nice to have another vehicle, and I'm enamored of Jeeps right now."

He shrugged. "You could buy one while we're at breakfast."

"Well, not AT breakfast, since I'd be really distracted. But after, maybe."

We wound our way down off the hill, headed for a decent breakfast. I decided to take a look at Tsillan Cellars restaurant. They advertised a very nice brunch, and that seemed like a good idea. It's out of town a ways and Cai and I rode along in companionable silence. The mood persisted through the brunch. I was driving, so left the wine to Cai, and he seemed to accept that with gusto. After eating, I felt a lot more like living, so we headed down to the lake. We got a couple of folding chairs out of Threepio and sat watching the early arrivals appear. It was fairly cool in the morning but tended to get much hotter as the day wore on.

Cai glanced over at me. "So, I feel like a fool today."

"Why's that?"

"You know why, Jane."

"Well, yes, I do. But I like to hear myself being vindicated out loud."

He crowed to the heavens, "She was right ... she was riiiight!"

It was exhilarating - also I felt stupid.

"Ok, ok, that's enough."

"I was just getting started."

"That's what I was worried about."

We stared off across the lake and watched the bathers arrive. The dock started getting busy as the teens filtered in, still waking up.

I took a breath. "No, she's not real."

He glanced at me, then at the lake again. "I know."

I glared at him. "What do you mean, you know? You just admitted I was right!"

"Well, you are right. About her being a real person. But I know she's not inhabiting a real body."

"You're splitting hairs, my dear."

He grinned. "I know."

I shook my head. "You're an enigma, Cai Shun."

"I have to be, I'm Asian."

"Sounds kind of racist."

"Not if I'm talking about myself."

"Jury's out on that one."

He frowned at me. "Do you know why I know her body isn't real?"

"No. I was actually wondering why you're so sure."

"You were distracted by her actions - but I was watching all of her. When she kissed Laney's forehead, most of her feet and legs dissolved into thin air. It was like watching a pair of legs that ended at the calves."

"Oh, really. I'll have something to definitely razz her about, then."

He looked doubtful. "I suppose. Are you sure it's safe? She must be very powerful."

"It's safe. Although I did see a family who has a full-grown tiger living with them. Assuring the internet it's all safe, that the tiger is just one of the family. So, yes, it's safe. Until it's not." I grinned at him. "I love taking chances."

"I know."

"Wanna go back to the house and meet Olive for real? And see her ... house?"

"It's what I've been hoping you'd say ever since I handed over that bit of glass to you. Free and clear, I must point out. But I think you owe me anyhow."

Soberly, "Yes. We do. More than you have any idea of. Let's head back. It's getting hot and crowded now, anyway."

We made our way back up to Threepio, tossed the chairs in and set off home. We wound up the hill to the house, and I was pleased to see the smartcar there.

We got out of the van and I patted the smartcar. "This is a spaceship."

Cai looked it over. "A million miles to the gallon?"

"Something like that. I must say you seem to take everything in stride."

"I'm reeling in my mind, I'm just hiding it from you."

Olive came out and stood in the drive not far from us. "So it's that way, is it? I thought he was onta me. I could feel 'im spike last night when he looked in my direction. And I can verify that he's reelin'. He does an excellent job of fakin' it, though." She walked over to him. "Are you ok, sweetie? I'm not dangerous, I promise. And I'd kiss you, but I'm not really up to it yet."

Cai's composure finally broke, but he handled it well, smiling at her and saying "A life without danger is no life at all. I'm very pleased to meet you for ... real ... Olive."

She glanced at me. "Has he got a strong stomach, ya think?"

"Probably. He's pretty well controlled. He won't let himself barf all over."

She smiled at Cai. "Want a ride in my car?"

He took a long shuddering breath, but said simply, "Yes, please."

"Olive, let me know when you're back. I'll meet you downstairs."

"Yassuh, boss."

I smirked at her and stuck out my tongue. "Good thing I like you." Then to Cai, "Be ready, she'll try to make you toss your cookies. Just remember, you can always close your eyes and think of England. Or Lhasa, perhaps."

He nodded. For some reason that few words of assurance made him look worse, but he marched over and got in the car.

"Olive? Make sure you play it straight until you can get away clean. I really feel like Mother is watching."

She nodded, then opened the door of the car and slid in. It backed sedately out of the driveway. I watched as they drove away, the tires crackling on the gravel. I wonder how she does it all. I never really thought to ask, but maybe I'll have to get a crash course on "how stuff works."

I yelled inside that I was back, then I pulled out a lounger and lay down on the front lawn to relax. After a bit, Bailey came outside and saw me and pulled one up next to me. Finally, Laney came out, still looking grumpy, and did the same. We all lay there in the afternoon sun, browning and drowsing and hardly saying a word. After a couple hours, Olive and Kai came back. Olive came over and pulled out a chair and lay down next to Laney's lounge. Cai picked his way back up the walkway and past us, hardly seeming to see us.

Olive grinned at me. "I know we were gonna meet downstairs, but Cai seemed to be in need of some rest after our ride."

"Uh huh. I figured that when I saw him. Tomorrow's soon enough for a tour of the facilities. And Laney looks like she's more interested in relaxing than showing off her computer systems."

Laney gave me a drowsy nod and closed her eyes again. Olive winked at me. Life is good. All that relaxing tired us out, and after a while, the crowd began to dwindle. Laney and Bailey went to Bailey's house, Olive went inside to do Olive things. I have no idea what she does, but probably study technical manuals and Kit's copious notes. Just about sunset, Cai came back out of the house, looking considerably more relaxed and refreshed than he was earlier. He pulled one of the chairs over and sat beside me.

"Looks like you passed the test again, Miss Bond."

"Mm, that's nice. What did I win?"

"Just more work, I'm afraid. I brought you a gift from the museum, though."

I put the lounger upright and sat back. "A gift? I tend to like gifts. Mostly."

Cai picked up a small package from the ground and handed it to me. It was actually gift wrapped, and looked like a man had done it. No offense, men, but most of you suck at gift wrapping. My advice? Use a pretty bag and maybe some tissue. Save yourself some grief and a few yards of scotch tape.

I unwrapped the item. It was a bit larger than a CD case, and about twice as thick. It wound up being a framed photograph of what looked like a moonscape. "It's very nice, Cai. Thank you."

"Oh, you are so polite, Miss Bond. Look closer at the picture."

I did so, looking pretty hard and finally I saw it. Just a glimmer, but once I focused on it, it was undeniably another bit of the same alien metal Kit and I spent a summer hunting.

"Interesting. And this is on the moon?"

"Yes. The dark side. I'm sure you know that China has an expedition there."

"I've seen some reports, but it's not getting a lot of coverage in the US news."

"I doubt this would get into the news. For one thing, I'm not sure anyone but myself has really taken note of it. I suppose the only reason I happened to see it was my sensitivity to the look and feel of that particular material. I thought you would be interested in seeing it, if you had indeed made use of the item I provided you."

I leaned back in my chair again and considered it. Olive asked me if she should come out and join us, and I asked her to wait, we'd be in shortly.

"Mister Shun, would you like to follow me?"

"My heart knows no bounds of the joy it would find in doing so."

I snorted. "Oh, I bet that one wins all the lady's hearts."

A smirk on the face of a man of Cai Shun's age and composure is completely undignified.

Cai followed me into the house, down the stairs and I showed him around the conference room. Then I showed him Bailey's office. Then I showed him my office. I got a little more reaction out of him with each one, especially my office. It was currently showing the same scene we had just left, but it was obviously daytime, 89 degrees and the sounds of birds and children laughing was fully audible. He looked over the hill and down to the now-familiar lake scene and shook his head.

"Amazing."

"Oh, this is just the opening show, Cai."

We went back to the main room and through the invisible door, the platform 9¾ door that isn't really there and can't be. We came out into the garage under the field, with its seeming acres of perfectly white, perfectly clean space. Olive got up from one of the comfortable chairs arrayed in various spaces. She came over and greeted us, then bowed to Cai.

"I guess y'all know what I am, now?"

"I believe I do, Miss Olive."

"Well, that's nice. I was gettin' tired of pretendin with you."

"You were doing a fine job of pretending, Miss Olive."

"Oh, cut the crap and call me Olive. You're too much a part of the family to call me anything else."

Cai bowed and said, "Of course, Olive. It's a pleasure to meet you."

"The pleasure is all mine, Cai. I just wish I could kiss them fingers of yours or something, you're one sexy male."

Cai actually blushed. A 70-year-old man, and he blushed. "I am unable to find a response, Olive. Thank you."

She laughed delightedly. "He's a treasure, ain't he, Jane?"

"He is indeed."

"Should we show him what the part he gave us does?"

"I think that's a perfect idea, Olive."

"Cai, you got any special heroes in your life? People with talent or great warriors, or sexy women?"

Cai went still a bit, then said, "A windhorse symbolizes the human soul and when used as a flag, blesses all who come near."

Olive nodded, appeared to think a moment, then said, "Hold out your hands in front of you. Be prepared for something quite heavy."

Cai looked puzzled, but held out his hands as instructed. A dense fog seemed to flow in around his hands, then slowly it coalesced into a small bronze horse, with wings and a cargo of some sort of perhaps feathers riding on the saddle.

From his expression and the way his arms moved, it appeared to weigh several pounds. I said, "You can put it down on the counter there, Cai, if you wish."

Slightly dazed, he complied, putting its base on the counter where he stood looking at it. "It's beautiful, Olive. But how did you ... you made it just now?"

"I searched the internet to find the most representative sample of the 'wind horse' that you spoke of. Then I simply made it happen. Cai, everything you see in this room was the direct result of the part you gave Jane. It was the missing piece of the puzzle and allowed me and my predecessor to create everything else that followed."

Cai nodded slowly, sinking into an available chair. "I had no idea. I just knew it belonged to Jane."

Olive sank into the chair across from him, and I sat next to him.

"It's a lot to take in, Cai. Can I get you tea?"

"That would be wonderful."

"Olive, can you provide us with tea set that might be appropriate for this meeting? It's entirely possible that Cai may want to keep it as a souvenir."

Olive grinned. "I sure can." And she did - a complete silver tea set slowly appeared on the counter next to the wind horse.

I picked up the set and brought it over to where Cai was sitting, placing it on the coffee table in between the chairs. I poured tea for Cai, and we all sat and had tea and the excellent tea cakes that Olive "made". Oh, and while Olive had hers plain, Cai and I both put a large amount of cream and sugar in ours.

After sitting for a while and staring at the tea set, I remembered the picture. I went back upstairs and got it, brought it back down and handed it to Olive. She glared at me as it fell through her to the chair.

"Y'all crazy, woman?"

I laughed and nodded. "I guess I am. It's hard to believe sometimes that your body isn't what it appears. I guess it's lucky we haven't done that sort of thing before.

She smirked and said, "Let me show you something." And with that, she reached down through her legs and carefully picked up the picture and raised it to her eyes. "I've been working out. I can't do much yet, but it doesn't exhaust my resources to do it now like it did yesterday."

"Wow, that's great, Olive!"

Cai just looked on in amazement, he wasn't fully up on Olive to realize what a breakthrough this was.

Olive was looking intently at the photograph. "I can see from the patterns and the lighting where this is, so I can take us to it without much issue. Very little has changed on the moon even over the time since my data samples, so unless there was a meteor strike or the like, it should not be an issue. However, it puzzles me where it would have come from. Kit blew the ship up over Montana, there should be no way that a part of the ship could have arrived in that area of the moon. I suppose it's theoretically possible for a part of have been launched so hard that it could have gone into a slow orbit around the moon until caught and dragged in by the moon's gravitational field. However, this is so much a long shot as to be almost impossible. We'll have to get it and bring it back for thorough analysis."

She dropped back into dialect, "If y'all think that's a good idea."

Cai looked a little at sea. "Who is Kit?"

"Oh honey, keep up. Kit was the AI who mos' killed Jane here with his 'speriments. He's gone and I done took over."

If anything, Cai looked even more confused. I decided I'd give it a try. "What she means, Cai, is that the former AI that ran the ship had some conflicts with being human, and he wound up losing track of some important things. He was taken offline for assessment and training. Olive has taken over his position."

Olive muttered, "S'wat I said." She got up and placed the picture carefully on the table, then sat again. Though subtle, I could see that she de-materialized her hands after sitting.

"I suppose it doesn't really matter for the purpose at hand. We need to discuss what we'll do and how. Cai, did you bring me this with the idea I'd be able to do something with it, or was it just a curiosity thing?"

Cai seemed to be recovering from the hits he'd taken over the last few minutes. He said, "I'm not completely sure, Jane. But I know if you don't find a way to acquire it, if the Chinese government gets it, it will simply vanish and never be seen again. We know from our tests that it can't be tested in any way - at least not that we were able to find."

"That was my thought, Cai. I don't see any reason for us to not make an attempt to retrieve it from the moon. Olive?"

"I'm rarin' to go, Jane. Only reason I got for not going already is that I can't pick it up once I get there. I can only have hands right here inside th' workroom."

"All right, then I guess we're of one accord. We'll start making plans to get there as quickly as we can. For one thing, we want to make sure it's not gone when we step out to grab it!"

CHAPTER FOURTEEN

Vegas Calling

Bailey was sitting in her office. She wasn't quite sure what was going on, but apparently Cai had brought something of much interest to Jane and Olive, and they were making plans.

Bailey was feeling just a little left out and useless, since it didn't seem that she was part of that at all. It was just a few days before Laney would be leaving for Las Vegas, probably never to return, and Bailey was casting about, looking for something interesting to pursue. She'd grown to appreciate Laney's intelligence, and after getting the stick out of her butt, she was interesting to be around. Laney would never be a warm, comfy person to spend time with, but she'd lost much of her ice-queen feel.

Bailey'd gone in the server room for awhile, but after getting a glare when she was standing in front of a rack that Laney wanted access to, she'd decided to go back in her office.

Bailey's phone rang, and while she figured it was yet another spam caller from an unfamiliar number, she still had to answer it since it was nominally the company's phone now, or at least it was the number she'd been giving out for Bailey and Bond's business line. Which made little sense, but she'd thought it was logical at the time.

"Bailey and Bond Investigations, Bailey speaking."

"Good morning, Ms. Bailey, please hold for Mister Carstead."

Bailey was tempted to hang up, but she'd played the hold game as an executive, it was probably poetic justice that she was on the other end of it now. It was only a few seconds though, so it wasn't a power ploy.

"Ms. Bailey, Howard Carstead here. How are you this morning?"

"I'm well, Mister Carstead - what can I do for you?"

"I understand you have some firsthand knowledge of winning at Roulette in Vegas. We'd like to hire you to look at some video and let us know what you think."

Bailey chuckled, "Well, Mister Carstead, simply winning at Roulette doesn't make me an expert in anything except luck, now does it?"

Carstead chuckled right back. "Of course not, Ms. Bailey. We just thought you might be interested. We'd be happy to pay you double your quoted rates, and it's just for watching some videos."

"You drive a hard bargain, Howard. Send them over - I'll turn you over to our IT person to handle the technical aspects."

"Perfect, thank you, Ms. Bailey."

Bailey transferred him to Laney's phone, giving her a heads-up as to what he wanted. About 30 minutes later, Laney came into her office and said, "Boss, I think you should look at this."

Bailey got up and headed into the conference room, where there was a video paused. Laney started it up and Bailey could see herself sitting at the slot machines. She was playing and Bailey remembered she'd lost a bunch, but gained it back - at least mostly. Suddenly she saw the camera zoom in and her head twitched, and she said something. A bit later, she got up and moved to a different machine. She moved several times, and the camera picked her up at different locations across the casino until she stopped at the

Roulette wheel. She started playing. After losing a particularly large bet, she stopped and seemed to be standing still. She gave a slight nod. And then she started winning. She won the next 17 bets, letting it ride each time. After the 17th win, she held up her hands and smiled. She left a very generous tip with the croupier, and then security came over and helped her carry her winnings. There was a label that appeared at the bottom of the screen - "cashed out 1.4 million". The video ended.

Laney looked at her with her mouth open. "You won 1.4 million in Vegas at the Roulette wheel?"

Bailey shrugged. "It was only about $700,000 after taxes."

"You won at Roulette seventeen times in a row!"

"I'm lucky sometimes."

Laney looked at her with her hands on her hips. "How did you do it?"

Bailey glared at her. "I just got lucky."

"I live in Vegas. No one gets that lucky."

Bailey simply walked away from her, back to her office. She mulled over the situation. It was untenable, but she couldn't see any option. She called Carstead. After running the gamut of secretaries, he came on the line.

"Ah, Ms. Bailey. It's good to hear from you again, and so soon."

"Thank you, Mister Carstead."

"So, what did you think of our bit of entertaining video?"

"I thought it was amazing that luck just came out of the air and that woman won all that money. Truly amazing. What did you think, Mister Carstead?"

"Oddly enough, I was of the same viewpoint, Ms. Bailey. Still, it would be well if we could find a way to ensure against that sort of luck happening again, don't you think? A completely foolproof way for anyone to simply walk into one of our establishments and take us to the cleaners. That's patently bad luck, no matter how you look at it. Well, at least from our standpoint. No equipment, no signs, no telltales. I wonder what it would take to nip this luck in the bud? Is that possible, Ms. Bailey?"

Bailey looked almost startled. "I rather thought you'd just show up and make sure the luck ... went away."

Carstead sounded amused. "No, we don't do that sort of thing anymore, Ms. Bailey. It's a business like any other. Of course, we'd object strenuously if someone was to show up at one of our establishments and have that much luck again. And we'd have to register our objections with you, Ms. Bailey. Through the courts, of course."

"Of course."

"Your associate, Ms. McDaniels?"

"Yes? She's only been working with us for a short time, Mister Carstead. She really knows nothing of our company."

"I'm aware of that, Ms. Bailey. I'm also aware that Jane Bond, the other half of Bailey and Bond, is likely on the verge of being related to her. And that Ms. McDaniels is graduating as a security consultant next year."

Hesitantly, "Yes, that's true."

"We'd like to hire her, Ms. Bailey. Offer a full ride scholarship to UNLV or another college of her choice and then, when she graduates, she goes to work for us. At a VERY good salary. Company car. Travel. Housing. All paid for by the company, of course."

Faintly, "Of course."

"Does that sound like a possibility, Ms. Bailey?"

"It sounds like a hostage situation to me."

Carstead laughed, and it sounded like he actually meant it. "Oh, Ms. Bailey, you've watched far too many late-night movies. We simply want an employee with connections. We feel that we've found that in your associate. And don't worry, she will work at her job. She will be exactly what she's trained and spent so much time in school for. And we'll cut years off her career path. How is this a 'hostage situation'?"

Bailey ground her teeth together. "I'll speak to her about it."

"Oh, I'd have expected nothing less."

"Good bye, Mister Carstead."

"Good bye, Ms. Bailey"

The connection went. Bailey sat at her desk and seethed. After a few minutes of seething, Laney nervously stepped into her office.

"How bad is it?"

"It's bad. They want to offer you a job. Full scholarship. College of your choice. Company car, vacations, hookers at your beck and call. "

"Hookers?"

Bailey ground out, "You know what I mean."

"I accept."

"You accept what?"

"Whatever he's offering. I'll take it. It's what I wanted, and it's being offered on a silver platter."

"With knives sticking out all over."

"Bailey. I live in Las Vegas and have all my life. I know how it works. And it usually works with people like me getting a job cleaning game machines out for the first ten years of our careers."

"You were eavesdropping."

"Of course I was eavesdropping! I'm the security consultant, do you not think I have access to every camera and listening device in this entire building?"

"Good point."

"Call him back!"

"I can't call him back, we'd sound desperate."

"I AM desperate. This is exactly what I dreamed of, but it was impossible. Now, thanks to whatever you did to screw with the Las Vegas establishment, it's coming true. Call him back!"

Bailey muttered as she dialed the phone, "I was just lucky ... "

Laney snorted and rolled her eyes.

This time, the time between her call and his answer was almost instantaneous.

"Good day, Ms. Bailey."

"Good day, Mister Carstead."

"I take it you've thought over my offer?"

Through her teeth, Bailey ground out, "Yes, we're interested."

"I thought you might be. You never took advantage of many of your high-roller comps or privileges, Ms. Bailey. Why don't you and Ms. McDaniels fly down at our expense, stay at the Aria, have a good time on the town, and look over our operation. I believe Ms. McDaniels will have no qualms about accepting our offer."

"Send me the information, Mister Carstead. We'll discuss it and get back to you."

Carstead laughed once again, "As you wish. Ms. Bailey. Er ... Ms. Bailey ... "

"Yes?"

"May the Odds be always in your Favor."

Bailey hung up the phone, barely cracking the cradle at all.

"Did he actually quote a movie to you?"

Bailey growled, "Yes. Yes, he did."

Laney grinned. "Makes me like him more. I wonder if he's single."

Bailey made a moue. "He quoted it wrong."

CHAPTER FIFTEEN

Time away

I got the feeling that something was up with Laney and Bailey, but I had no idea what it was. Sadly, I was so busy trying to keep my other two associates reined in that I could barely keep track of my own life, let alone theirs.

Olive and Cai grew thick as thieves over the next few days. I listened to some of their plotting and planning, but they were in their own world. Still, someone had to keep them from enacting too many of their hare-brained schemes. And then they drew me back into it again. Olive wouldn't let Cai go to the moon with her - she was too worried about his heart. Evidently, he had a weakness. It seems to me the time to be concerned about his heart was when she was ramrodding him around the sky, but apparently she didn't know about it, then. It almost caused a rift between them, but she pointed out that he'd had to come home from their excursion and take heavy medication just to keep from dying - something I'd had no idea of when he stumbled past us that evening. I kicked myself for that, but of course, hindsight is always - well, you know.

At any rate, the upshot of it all was that I was going to the moon along with Bailey. And Bailey was gone to Vegas with Laney. Bailey didn't give me the details, but it seemed that her winning at the Roulette wheel had not gone unnoticed (which didn't surprise me, I was still watching for tommy guns) and they'd offered Laney a job. While Bailey seemed to be pretty steamed about it, Laney was over the moon (so to speak) about it. And so, they were going to Las Vegas for the week and would leave Laney off there to start school. Which meant we couldn't go to the moon until after Bailey got back, and of course that made both Cai and Olive pretty antsy. I swear, sometimes they're both the same age, I have to keep reminding them to use their words.

I thought it was funny - that Bailey's windfall turned into such a windfall for Laney, too. Dale was pretty over the moon as well, at the risk of using that metaphor too much. Evidently working for MGM was a big deal. I had no idea it was the biggest casino operation in the world. Or at least I didn't before. I got the negative aspects of it from Bailey, followed by the rainbow unicorn aspects of it from Laney fifteen minutes later. It made me crazy.

So. I decided I'd take a vacation. Just me and Dale. He got time off work, I got time away from the family, and we both got to spend time together. Talk about win-win. Olive dropped me at a car dealership in Missoula - I was going to buy that Jeep and drive it home after my vacation with Dale.

I found a nice used five-year-old Wrangler in yellow. Low mileage and nice looking. I know, my budget is essentially unlimited, but it's never encouraged me to waste money. I just hope Threepio doesn't wind up too jealous! I'm withholding a name until I find out more about him (or her) but I'm leaning toward Jerry. Don't ask me why, it just popped in. I hope I don't wind up changing that to Lemon before the trip is over, but so far, so good.

Dale was happy to see me, and we spent a glorious week scouting around the area. A giant 4-door pickup isn't particularly conducive to "hiking" into the back country, so while Dale knows every little byway in the area, it's not something he does in his off time. I suppose I was probably tormenting him by forcing him into basically spending time in his work mode - on vacation. But that's the breaks. And he gets kisses, so it can't be all bad.

We dropped in at the Wagon Wheel a few times. Laura is just as she always is. She berated us for missing the July 4th Choteau celebration, but gave us free fries anyhow, so she wasn't too mad.

Relaxed and refreshed after the week away, we decided to drive back to Washington together. Olive could always bring Dale back after the trip. Jerry is relatively comfortable, and the trip was relatively uneventful. We arrived back about the same time as Bailey. We'd decided in the necessity of having her return home on an airplane since having her simply vanish out of Vegas might be signaling the wrong things to either my mother or Laney's Vegas sugar daddy.

Speaking of my mother, I haven't heard anything from her. While that's not unusual, she's not one to give up without a fight. I'd better have Olive extend some long-range scanners to make sure mother isn't watching. I considered calling her Big Mother, but decided that might have too many connotations and turn it into an insult. And it would also be way too accurate.

For some reason I'm worried about this trip to the moon. Since we'll be basically yanking something out from under the Chinese government's nose, it feels like a dangerous event. But we'll be quickly in, quickly out - what could go wrong. Right?

CHAPTER SIXTEEN

Oh, the humanity

I t had not entirely escaped my attention that the idea of leaving Cai and Olive together alone might not be the best course. However, they were both adults (although that's debatable) and I figured the house was pretty much indestructible and Olive could rebuild anything that came to harm. At least that was my rationale.

The error in my thinking came to my attention shortly after I returned from vacation. Olive offered me a ride down to town to pick up supplies. I thought she might be feeling a little bummed over a new vehicle in the barn, but it turned out that wasn't so much the case. As I found out when she took my hand in hers and kissed it. I looked at her, startled. She smiled and continued driving.

"My goodness! Well, congratulations! You've really been working hard ... but if this is what you want, I guess I can't say anything about it."

"Well, actually, you can say quite a lot about it, Jane. I've taken your permission to expand my capabilities and run with it. Quite a ways. So far, I'm still just a shell, but it's enough to make things far more possible. I cooked pancakes! For real, I mean. I can't eat them, but I cooked them, and Cai ate them without complaining. Of course, he doesn't complain much about much.

I said quietly, "How far do you intend to take this project, Olive?"

She whispered, "I don't know." She turned and looked at me, almost defiantly, and much louder. "What do you think, Jane? You've always told me an Kit both that we's people, just in a dif'rnt body. Do you believe that?"

"I do, Olive."

"But ...?"

"No buts. Beyond the but that says being human isn't all it's cracked up to be. That there is misery and heartache attached."

"So, that really means that you don't and never did think of me as human."

I had to sigh. "Olive, I've never thought of you as anything other than human. And I already said that before - about heartache and pain. You will have heartache and pain, love, no matter what body you're in."

Olive sat back disconsolately. "Nothing is free?"

"Nothing is free."

She leaned against me, the cloud of bots that is her projection brushing against my skin like fine silken cobwebs. "I want to be human, Jane. All human. No matter how much pain it causes me. Pain makes humans - human. Isn't that right?"

I took a breath. "Yes, in the end, we are sculpted by our pains. Our failures, our foibles and sometimes our successes. They all come together to make a human."

She nodded.

We sat there silently for a while, then she rose and went up the path to the house - but halfway she turned and said, "Good night, Mom."

"Good night, Olive."

CHAPTER SEVENTEEN

On being a Moonie.

I woke up the next morning relaxed, refreshed and ready to eat tigers. Or at least tiger striped pancakes. I could smell something like that cooking, so decided to have a trip downstairs. I pulled on some shorts and a tee shirt and headed for the kitchen.

I was greeted by an interesting sight. Olive was juggling the pancake turner between pancake turns. Then she slid it under a pancake and tossed it to Cai, who was waiting expectantly. She caught sight of me and grinned. "Grab a plate, I'll toss you breakfast!"

I got a plate down from the cupboard as Bailey walked in. I gave her a plate too, and we both sat and stared at Olive. She was back to juggling again, but the most disconcerting thing was that when she popped out from behind the island, the bottom half of her was missing. It was really strange, since she was moving like she had legs, but ... she didn't. Also hips. It was very disconcerting to see her walking around, but without legs.

"Go back behind the island again, you're making me dizzy."

She rolled her eyes, but scurried back behind and I felt better.

"Thanks, sweetie."

She beamed. "Pancakes for both of you?"

We both nodded and she set about pouring batter. I glanced at Cai, but he only had eyes for her. I have to admit it was entertaining, her shifting about in the kitchen, handling the ladles and turners with aplomb. A bit later, she flipped pancakes in the pan, then a golden-brown moment after that, she flipped them to us, one to me and another to Bailey. I like plenty of butter, so I got up and grabbed the butter. Bailey put some on but she's a wimp with butter. It's one of my few extravagances, so I take it to town.

I forked into the cake and took a bite. "Olive, that's amazing! Where did you learn all this?"

She giggled excitedly, "You really like them? I made about five thousand of them virtually before I felt confident enough to bring them out here."

"They are fabulous!"

Cai and Bailey echoed my sentiments, and we all ate in happy gluttony. After finishing the cooking, Olive reformed her lower half and sat with us, eating virtual pancakes with a virtual plate - and real gusto. I noticed that her pancakes had at least as much butter on them as mine. I'm teaching her right, apparently.

After we all finished and had done the obligatory leaning back and groaning, I said, "Well, today is the day, I guess."

Cai looked a little grumpy, but everyone else reacted with happy looks.

"So, what's the plan?"

Cai muttered, "Go to the moon, get the thing, and come back."

"My goodness, someone woke up on the wrong side of the bed this morning."

"I've spent a good part of my life wondering about that piece of ... whatever it is. And now that I have a chance to go to the moon on a spaceship I helped FIND, I'm not allowed to."

Bailey spoke up at that point, "I'm more than willing for Cai to take my place, he deserves a chance to do what he's always wanted to."

"He's got a bad heart, it might kill him just going there," Olive said. "The lighter gravity might stress him into an attack."

I shrugged. "If Bailey doesn't really care that much about going, maybe Cai should be the one to go with us, Olive. This is his one chance to do this. You should be familiar with impossible dreams if any of us is."

"Fine! Let him go along and ... and let him die if it happens!"

There were tears flowing down her cheeks, and even though I knew it might be artifice, I suddenly wondered if she felt something for him - something more than just friends. It crossed my mind too as to what her little tattoo said - had it been 'Jane', then 'Laney' and now 'Cai"?

We all sat in silence, and then Olive threw up her hands in disgust. "All right, I understand. But this won't be on me if anything happens." She stalked out of the room, leaving all of us staring uncomfortably at each other.

I gathered Bailey in with my eyes, "Let's go get snacks and drinks for the trip. And you can have whatever's left to pig out on while you're here."

"Yeah. Alone. No one to be with me. What happens if I get lonely?"

"Watch TV. Or the beach. Or you could sit and whine and feel sorry for yourself. Or sunbathe, it'll be a great day for it."

Bailey glared at me, then stuck her tongue out. "I'll get changed."

As I'd said, it was a great day for it, the weather was perfect. So far it was sitting at about 85 at noon, and that pointed to it being no more than 90 or 95 later. Heck, if I wasn't going to the moon, I'd be laying out myself!

We trekked out to the barn and got in the Jeep. It was large enough that we had to park it outside, maybe I'd build a lean-to for it, or the like. A carport, I guess. We wound our way down the hill and onto the main road below, rolling into downtown Chelan a few minutes later. The weather was so perfect that many of the people were off enjoying the day and not bothering with touristing duties like picking up groceries and buying liquor.

We wandered through Safeway, looking at this and that and just having a nice conversation together. I liked having a family such as Cai and Olive had become in such a short time, but I missed my alone time like I'd had before all this happened. We're so seldom happy with "today", are we?

"Bailey, dear, have you missed the Seattle life yet?"

"Nah, I'm reveling in being able to sleep in, wear whatever I want and drink whatever I want whenever I want. Maybe someday I'll miss it, but not yet. Also, thanks to your bit of seed money I have enough additional cash in my retirement account to put off having to consider another job for some time yet."

I rolled my eyes. "You have a job, Bailey." I frowned. "You are collecting a paycheck, aren't you?"

"Of course not. I'm not DOING anything."

"You definitely need to be collecting a paycheck though, Bailey. You're part of the startup, you did the research and once we get past this ... this adventure we're currently involved in, we'll be up to our asses in detective clients."

"That sounds promising, although I'd want them to be good looking if they're going to be next to my ass."

"I'll keep that in mind when I go hunting for clients. Maybe we can put that in the ad."

"Put in the ad that they'll be close to my ass?"

I snorted. "No, but I guess we could do that. If we put a picture of it, we'd get a lot more clients. But I'm not sure they'd be looking for detective work."

"Mm, yeah. On consideration, let's leave my ass out of it."

We picked up wine, some vodka, a little bottle of Sailor Jerry's rum (mostly 'cause I liked the picture) and some various mixers and other liquors. I'd thought we were getting trip snacks, but it seemed that Bailey had more in mind than that.

"You know, we could probably find a way to get us all to fit in the ship."

"No way, I'm looking forward to a whole night alone! I'll binge on whatever HGTV has on tonight and drink my way through a lot of Rum and Cokes."

"I think that's the wrong kind of rum for that, sweetiecakes."

"Are you thinking about my ass again?"

"Heaven forbid."

"Most likely."

We picked up more rum. More chips. More salsa. Geez, at this rate, I was going to have to go the gym twice a day rather than twice a week. After paying the national debt for the "road snacks" we headed back home.

When we rolled in the driveway, I could see that Olive and Cai had made up. She was sitting in her chair in a bikini and he was sitting in his, working at not staring. We stopped at the house and unloaded, Cai helping with the boxes.

I frowned at him, reminded him of his heart, but he said, "It's mostly in her imagination. It's never been an issue, no one's ever told me to cut back on anything."

At that point I dropped it. He's an adult, and in charge of his own life. I doubt I'd be much of a friend if I kept sniping at him.

We unloaded the car and loaded up the fridge and the cupboards and sat back for a well-deserved lunch of chips and salsa. We virtuously said we'd wait until at least 3 to start drinking. Or that's what Bailey said - the rest of us figured we'd be on the moon by then. Or at least on the way.

After sitting around talking, laughing, eating and drinking for a couple hours, Olive finally said, "Hey, are we going to the moon or are you people just chickening out?"

After a few chicken imitations from Bailey, I admitted I was a little scared by the thought. I mean, yeah, I'd been to the moon before, but it was only about 45 minutes and it was by accident anyhow. And I was naked for part of it, which wasn't much fun.

Cai was curious about the naked part, so of course Olive filled him in, and he had a good laugh. But the upshot was that he was nervous as well, so I felt better. After the four of us got into a stare-down, I finally just got up and lead the way into the garage. Olive had moved the ship there earlier to facilitate loading and leaving undetected.

I vanished into the shower/bathroom/changing room and came out in my skinsuit. Cai didn't whistle, but I could tell he was tempted. I'd forgotten he'd never seen me ... erm ... "dressed" in it before. Olive pointed him toward the closet on the ship and he looked inside - like a kid at Christmas he pulled out a black male-style skinsuit of his own and left to put it on.

Pretty soon I saw the changing room door open, but nothing happened. It just stayed like that. Then he poked his head out, saw us all looking and ducked back inside.

I yelled, "Hey, mister moon man, come out here. If I can do it, you can do it!"

A little shamefacedly he stepped out into the hallway and seeing him from the outside made me blush at what I must look like. I mean, it was reasonably tasteful, but it sure didn't leave much to the imagination. Dale had just flat out refused to wear his, and considering what it didn't cover (basically the old style men's skinsuit was just a speedo and a lot of black paint) I didn't really blame him. Of course, I was used to wearing next to nothing in public, and I was showing less in my skinsuit than in most of my bikinis. But Cai - he'd shown up wearing a three-piece suit. It had taken him a couple days to get used to even wearing jeans. Shorts had taken another week after that.

Anyhow, a little chivvying around and we wound up standing next to each other. A slightly tipsy (since it was nearly after three by then) Bailey took pictures of us and then we went into the ship and sat while we waited for Olive to do the cross-checks and make sure that the runway was ... never mind. She didn't do any of that. I swear, that flock of seagulls must be

149

getting thinned out by now, since that's the only way that Olive seems to know how to launch - straight up at least a million miles an hour. Maybe she just doesn't like seagulls. My Steve used to call them rats with wings - although I thought some of them were kind of pretty.

We opted to take the scenic route this time, since Cai had never been to the moon before. And here I am talking like an old hand, and I've only been there once.

Olive took things a good deal more gently this time. I suspect it was from her concern for Cai, but it might have been that she wanted to update her own maps. I have no idea and I'm not going to speculate. At any rate, we cruised along, looking at the various landing sites on the moon. It was a kind of zig zag fashion as we visited Apollo sites 12, 14, 16, 11, 17 and then all the way up to 15. We took a close look at the various space junk left behind on the moon, and considered a ride in a lunar rover when Olive assured us she could recharge it on a temporary basis. However, we decided it would be like pushing over a gravestone to move the rovers around, so we left them unmolested, to Olive's disgust.

We poked our heads over the top of the rise where Olive had told us to expect the part we were looking for. Of course, when we came over the top, there were already visitors there. It was only automated cameras of course, but still, it would be hard to cover up footprints, dust and other activities suddenly appearing within the view of the cameras. Cai said that in his experience they had shut down the cameras to conserve batteries after several hours of running each day, and the fact that the sun swung around and gave them nothing but glare on the screen probably had something to do with that as well. I suppose there was really no big reason why they'd leave them running, since what would you expect to change in the unchanging landscape of the moon? Except, of course, when interlopers appear in invisible spaceships.

Not willing to just sit and wait, Cai and I decided to try out the suits. Or at least Cai's suit, since mine seemed to be in tip-top shape. We left the ship, and Olive followed us in her identical suit. I suppose she could have left footprints like we did, but she didn't bother. I think she was still miffed that I'd pulled rank and had taken Cai along.

We waved at each other, bounced up and down the hills in the one-sixth gravity, and in general made loonies of ourselves. The suits allowed us to talk back and forth, so we could hear the laughing and joking as we toured our bit of the moon. Finally tiring of playing in the dust we stopped and went back to sit in the ship.

There, we sat and gnawed at our fingernails. Figuratively speaking, of course, since we couldn't actually gnaw our fingernails through the skinsuits. We watched the cameras not watching us. After an hour or so of this, and of us being driven stir crazy, the cameras nosed down as they turned off and that was that. We had a free hand.

"Ok, I'm going to maneuver us in closer, it should be ... yes ... "

"Yes, what?"

"Yes, I see it. It's embedded in the wall. What a miracle that it just buried itself in there where we could see it."

"Han Solo would say 'I call it luck' but I dunno. Maybe we were meant to find it."

Cai said, "In my experience, there is no such thing as luck."

We both turned and looked at him.

"Hey, I am not THAT old. I like Star Wars too!"

We both grinned at each other, then turned back around to face the front.

Olive was watching as we flew closer - finally she said, "Imma gonna park us here. I can' get much closer without bein in the camera view. They could wake up and I can' cloak you two out there."

I scowled out over the landscape. "It's a couple hundred yards to the crater wall, so we should only take a couple minutes to get there. I guess it's

151

harder to walk on the moon though, so we should be prepared for that. Instead of just bouncing around maybe we should have taken a walk. Ever walk in 20% gravity before, Cai?"

"No, but I have taken some introductory classes. You can go in a pool of water with enough weight and it simulates much of the problems with low gravity. However, I have found that most of the problems I had in moving were caused by the suits. Here, our skinsuits are very flexible and are almost ... erm ... like being naked." He very pointedly didn't look at me when he said this.

"Uh huh. It feels weird to have the sand between your toes, or moon dust, I guess. I didn't notice all that much problem when we were dancing around out there, Cai."

We both took a breath at about the same time and looked at each other, laughing. Olive rolled her eyes, but I thought she was amused and probably stored it away as something human to do someday.

"Open the pod bay doors, Olive. Let's do this."

"We don't talk anymore after what happened."

I grinned again. "Thanks, Alexa."

In a robotty voice - "No problem."

So, with no further ado, we stepped out onto the surface of the moon. It wasn't bad at all walking, just had to remember to step carefully and not push off too hard or you wound up bounding around. I bounced too hard and ran into Cai, and we both wound up running THROUGH Olive, which pissed her off royally.

Even with the clowning around it only took a couple minutes to get to the wall. I could see the gadget stuck there. We all looked at it, none of us wanting to make the move. Finally, Cai and Olive said, in unison, "Take it, Jane."

I reached out for it and got a good grip. "It's one small pull for a man, one ..." Suddenly I couldn't breathe and my side lit up on fire like a hot poker had just slid through it.

CHAPTER EIGHTEEN

Or not.

Jane screamed and fell to the surface. She was suddenly stark naked and had a giant wound in her side, pumping out blood. Cai managed to get his hand over the wound, and wrestled her up into his arms, holding her. He began to run, but in his haste, he over bounced and hit the crater wall far from the ship.

He screamed, "Olive! Get the ship closer! Fast! She's bleeding out, and the vacuum is pulling it out even faster!"

Olive had become so human that instead of reacting like a computer, she reacted like a human and simply stood there, rooted.

Cai got back on course and started to run again, more on target this time. Olive managed to unfreeze and got the ship moving, and triangulated where Cai would land, so he wound up basically falling into the ship. Olive slammed the doors and got the cabin pressurized, but while Jane's side stopped gushing, it was still bleeding hard, and she was so pale.

Cai moved to one side and sat on the floor, and Olive pulled a heavy bandage out of thin air. She applied it to Jane's side, holding her breath that it would stick and plug up the wounds. There were two of them, one appearing to be the incoming wound and the other the exit. The incoming one was under Jane's lower ribs, the other coming out through one of the ribs in her back, a few inches up - whatever it was had gone straight through and left nothing but a hole behind.

The ship took off and broke all Olive's speed records getting back to earth. Her panicked human flight had smoothed out, and she was now thinking in the best computer fashion. Her trajectory brought the ship in over the U.S. and she opted for Seattle since it was closest. Also, Seattle is reputed to have one of the best emergency rooms in the country. She landed the ship in Seattle's HarborView emergency bay. She screamed at Cai to get Jane out of the ship so she could move it, but he just lay there and said nothing. Finally, after vital seconds she realized he wasn't conscious either. So, she materialized hands and began tugging Jane out the door. She managed to get her to the parking lot, grabbed Cai and dragged him out the door as well. She sent the ship away and with her last gasp of power, she screamed her lungs out through the open door of the emergency bay. Then she dissoluted, not enough power left even for the wisp.

Emergency room techs came boiling out of the door, finding an unconscious elderly man dressed in a wetsuit. Lying next to him was a naked woman apparently bleeding to death. For Harborview, this wasn't really that out of the ordinary and they got both of the patients through the doors post haste.

The woman's wounds were grave, and she'd lost a lot of blood. She also had burst capillaries in her eyes and swelling in some of her extremities, as if she'd come up from deep in the water without decompressing first. They started treating that, but of course it was second to the horrible wounds in her side.

The decompression was consistent with the man's clothing, as he was wearing some sort of high-tech wetsuit. Unfortunately, no one could ask him anything, as he'd suffered a heart attack. Their theory at this point was that the woman had brought the man up from a deep-water location in hopes of getting help for his heart problem. This theory didn't really hold water, so to speak, since how did they get to the emergency room, and the fact that neither of them was wet.

So, they went to work on the two, and the doctors didn't really care much about the anomalies in the story since they were far more interested in saving lives. Funny how that works. Gossip ran around the hospital, however, and it wasn't long before it was on the news complete with (artfully blurred) footage of the naked woman. She was attractive enough to make it sure this story got good play - how can you turn down this much chance to show nudity on the small screen? Ratings, baby, ratings.

Earlier that day, Bailey had been taking it easy. She'd alternated food and drink until she wasn't very sure which was which, so she decided she'd stop. She would never admit it to Jane, but she liked the Property Brothers almost as much as Jane did, and Bailey had found a whole cache of episodes on Jane's DVR. So, she binge-watched Jonathan and Drew and their antics, taking five or six weeks to bring people's dreams to life. It was something you could give your attention to, that. Finally, the food, the drinks and the Brothers took control and she fell asleep - waking up to the news playing when the DVR ran out. She almost clicked it off, and then started hyperventilating - that was Jane on the screen. A story about a Jane and John Doe couple who'd been admitted to Harborview an hour or two earlier. The woman had a large bleeding wound and the man had been very still. Beyond the clandestine smartphone footage, there'd been no comment from the hospital, but police were investigating. An appeal for anyone who knew the couple was given a number to call. All thought of sleep had gone, and the fog of alcohol had evaporated. Bailey dialed the number with shaking hands.

"Harborview, this is Lydia, how may I direct your call?"

"Th ... th ... I have - I know the woman on TV."

"I'm sorry, ma'am, woman on TV?"

"The naked woman that you just found in your driveway, with the man?"

"The ... OH! Yes, let me transfer you."

The line clicked and after a short wait, it began to ring.

"Nurse station six, this is Charlie, how may I help you?"

"I know the woman - the naked woman they just brought in, and the man with her."

"Yes, ma'am. What's your name, please?"

"Bailey McCallum."

"Could you spell that?"

Slightly annoyed, Bailey spelled it out, twice on the last name.

"And the location you're calling from?"

"Chelan, Washington."

"Date of birth?"

Bailey spluttered, "My friend is in your hospital dying, can we get this later?"

"No ma'am, date of birth please."

Fuming, Bailey said "July 12th, 1990"

"Do you have insurance, ma'am?"

"Do I ha ... listen, I want to talk to someone about the people that were brought in there. I need to know their condition and what's going on! Let me speak to your supervisor."

The voice grew several degrees cooler. "I am the floor supervisor, what may I help you with."

By now the fury had well overtaken Bailey. "Do you know Doctor Jon Frees?"

Bored voice, "Yes, of course I know Dr. Frees."

"Well, if you can't help me, put me through to him, or his secretary. Or possibly you'd rather I called him at home?"

Since Dr. Frees was the CEO of Harborview Hospital, the nurse thought better of her position. "I'll put you through to ICU, have a pleasant night."

Bailey thought, "A better day than you'll have tomorrow, bitch." but didn't say it out loud. Instead she said, "Thank you, Charlie."

The phone began to ring, it was answered with a cheery, "ICU, this is Carleen, how may I help you?"

"Carleen, I have information about the couple that was brought in earlier this evening - the naked woman and the man with her?"

"Oh my, yes. Let me take that down."

"All right. Her name is Jane Bond, she's 31, she lives in Chelan, Washington. His name is Cai Shun, he's a Tibetan national who's here visiting for a short time. If I go to the Chelan hospital, can I get her medical records released for you? Would that do any good?"

"I'm sorry, ma'am, probably not. HIPAA regulations make it hard for anyone to get those records released, but her name and the fact that she's not conscious will mean we should be able to gain access to them. Do you have a next of kin for her?"

Bailey gasped. "Is she dead?"

Carleen drew in a breath, "Oh, I'm so sorry. No, no - she's not dead. She's in critical condition, as is Mister Shun, but they are alive. But there are certain procedures that are very hard to take care of without permission from a guardian or a next of kin."

Bailey faltered. "I ... I don't know her mother or her father's name. They don't get along well and as far as I know her mother has never been to Chelan to see her. They are military people, maybe you can track them through that. Bond is her maiden name. As to Mister Shun, should I call the Tibet Embassy? Do ... do they even have an embassy?"

"I'm not sure of that, ma'am." Carleen seemed to be distracted for a moment, then she said, "I believe ... her mother is here."

Bailey drew a blank. "How ... how can her mother be there?"

Carleen whispered, "I don't know, but a large woman dressed in army fatigues is here. Does that sound like Ms. Bond's mother?"

Bailey sighed. "Yes, it does. I'll call the embassy if I can find one. And I'll be to Seattle soon. "

"Ma'am, can I get your name and a number to reach you at?"

"Oh - yes, of course, I'm sorry. Your nurse at the front desk was ..."

"Charlie?"

"Yes."

"Oh. Well, if I can get your name, I'll see what can do for Jane and her mother. And Mr. Shun, of course."

Bailey gave out her name and number and hung up. Now that the immediate threat was resolved, she was feeling like a wet noodle. And she also started thinking. "Where is Olive?" She ran downstairs, but the conference room was just a conference room. Jane's office remained locked, no matter how she pushed and pried on the door, and the door to the garage was simply nonexistent. Bailey's office let her in, but all it was ... was an office. And no amount of yelling Olive's name did anything at all. The enormity of it sank in, and it washed over Bailey. Jane and Cai nearly dead and Olive gone. And the random thoughts Jane had mentioned came unbidden, and echoed in her mind. "He's insane, you know." and "But the Mark VI is nearly insanity proof." And, finally, "But didn't he try to kill you?"

"Jane, what have you gotten yourself into ..."

Olive was having a rough night. Her dissolution had been nearly complete, but the ship had held onto a tiny amount of power in spite of her demanding all of it. As a result Olive was in ICU (figuratively speaking) just like the rest of her team, but she wasn't dead. The ship managed to gain small amounts of energy from the dust settling on its skin. With that, it landed and dug into the ground a bit and drew in enough dirt to make some more power. With that it had enough to limp home to Chelan, where it landed in its bay in the garage and began pulling real power from the main unit housed there. At some point, it brought Olive back online.

Olive woke and immediately formed her projection. She was so bound to having a body by now that she felt as if she didn't exist without it. Once that happened, she became conscious of Bailey yelling - screaming even. And ... crying? Waves of fear washed over her, and she started yelling too - screaming for Bailey.

She keyed open the garage door and ran through, finding Bailey standing on the other side, her fists raised.

Bailey jumped back and screamed at her, "What did you do to them? What happened?"

Olive held up her hands and started to weep. "It was an accident, a horrible accident." Then, brokenly, "Something ... the part we went after ... it seemed to come to life when Jane touched it, and it ... it went right through Jane when it flew away. It seemed to ... drain all the power from Jane's suit when she touched the artifact. I've never heard of a suit just dissipating like that."

Bailey stood down some in her righteous fear and indignation, "Oh. What happened to Cai?"

Sobbing, Olive said, "I'm not sure, but he carried Jane back to the ship and collapsed. I think he may have had a heart attack from the stress and exertion." She began hitting herself on the head, stuttering out, "I didn't even know he was hurt, I just thought he was sitting. I yelled at him to drag Jane out to the hospital and even got mad at him when he didn't say anything." Her words were punctuated by tears flying and hits to her head.

Bailey's heart went out to her. "Oh Olive, you did all you could. It's okay... shh shh ... hey, look at me..."

Olive's tear streaked face looked up at Bailey. "I killed them, Bailey. I need to go into shut down mode - reboot and reinitialize."

Bailey slapped her face. Of course, her hand went through, but it caught Olive's attention. "Stop that. You did nothing wrong. Accidents happen, love. Besides, last I heard a few minutes ago, they were both alive. Did you mean to hurt them?"

"Hurt them? Oh, no no, I love Jane. I've come to love Cai. I would never hurt them."

Gently, "Then stop this talk of rebooting or reinitializing. You're human, sweetie. You did all you could. Sometimes that's all we can do."

"Jane ... Jane said being human would cause heartache and pain. But I ... Bailey, I just didn't understand what she meant, I guess."

Bailey smiled sadly, "I think that's part of being human. Sometimes the only way we can keep living from day to day is to misunderstand or forget what it was to be human yesterday and start out again today."

Even with Olive's help, Bailey found it almost impossible to find anyone to call about Cai. Finally, she gave up and called the Tibet Museum. They assured her she'd done the right thing and would get in contact with Cai's family.

Bailey sat for a bit, considering plans. She hated to ask, but finally, "Olive, can you fly yet, take us to Seattle to see Jane and Cai?"

"Yes, I'm nearly back to full capacity. The poor ship limped along to get back here. I wasn't even conscious again until we had been here for a while."

"You - Olive, you sacrificed yourself for them? I didn't know that."

Olive gave her a strange look. "It wasn't even a question, Bailey. I'd give my life for Jane."

Bailey stared back for a moment. "Then, that makes you more human than a lot of humans."

Olive turned away uncomfortably. "We'd better get on board and get moving."

As the started up the ramp, they realized the blood from Jane's wound was still there.

Bailey looked a little faint. "So much blood. This is all from Jane? Was there even any left in her?"

"Not much, Bailey, not much."

They felt a little gruesome, like somehow they were profaning Jane to be wiping up her blood so casually, but it had to be done. They both knew that Olive-the-ship could have done it in one swipe, but somehow it was important they worked together on this. Finally, they had the floor and ramp clean, and the ... spatter ... wiped from the controls.

Olive wiped a spot from the vinyl seat and then nearly broke down. "Jane wanted cloth seats, but I ... I hadn't done it yet."

In an effort to defuse the situation, Bailey said, "See, procrastination pays off."

They looked at each other and broke into hysterical giggles. After they ran down, Olive took the ship up out of the garage and they headed for Seattle.

The trip to Seattle hardly lasted long enough for them to get any more morose. Bailey made the call to Dale, and he assured her he'd be on his way as soon as it was humanly possible. On arrival at Harborview, Olive hunted around for someplace to park the ship where she had a decent chance of seeing Jane. Finally, she just parked in a planter with nothing too much growing there and they debarked into ... bark. Seattle was cool and it had been raining earlier, but it was fairly clear now. They picked their way through the flower bed and went in through the main entrance.

Stopping at the front desk, they asked for Jane Bond's condition. They were told there was no information yet, and to feel free to have a seat in the waiting room.

At the waiting room, Bailey stopped, looked around and whispered an aside to Olive, "If Jane was here, she'd say there was an army of people waiting."

Olive smiled a bit. And indeed, there were no fewer than five people dressed in military fatigues, all sitting patiently in a row.

There were also three Asian men and a woman, all wearing black suits.

Bailey said to the room in general, "I'm Bailey McCallum. I'm Jane's best friend. I'm also a friend of Cai Shun. This is our friend Olive Daship. Are most of you here to see Jane or Mr. Shun?"

One of the Asian men stood and bowed to Bailey and Olive. "I am Dai Shun. I have come to see my father." He motioned to the others around him. "These are associates of my father's, who are also based in the Seattle area. We have come to offer him support and prayer."

Bailey bowed, with Olive following suit. "We are pleased and honored to meet you, Mr. Shun. We have become good friends with your father. He is a wonderful man and we pray along with you that he will be well."

One of the women in uniform stood. "I'm Jeannie Bond. Jane's my daughter. I'm pleased to meet you as well, Ms. McCallum, Ms. Daship. Joe, Jane's father, is on his way but he won't be here for a few hours." Bailey was surprised as she looked at Jeannie - the red-rimmed eyes told more of the story of her feelings than anything Bailey would have expected.

"No news at all?"

Dai and Jeannie shook their heads, nearly in unison.

Bailey and Olive took seats together near the others and they all proceeded to engage in the time honored tradition of waiting, drinking bad coffee and eating stale breakfast pastries. At midnight.

Olive leaned over to whisper in Bailey's ear, "When did I get th' last name of Daship?"

"It was the best I could come up with. What was I gonna say, no last name? I thought it was funny. I'm human, so shoot me. No one will ever really remember it, so change it if you want."

Olive rolled her eyes expressively. "I can't. It's ... stuck now."

"Jane says you named yourself, it's not HER fault you didn't give yourself a last name."

"Touche', I guess."

"I guess."

They lapsed into silence, Bailey finally pulling out her phone and reading something on her Kindle app. Olive simply sat, probably doing virtual pancake flipping. Or virtual human practice. Or thinking about the future Mr. (or Mrs.) Daship.

After a while, Jeannie moved over to sit next to Bailey. Bailey looked at her politely, "Hello, Ms. Bond."

Jeannie sighed. "I know, I'm a bitch. Get it over with, just say it out loud so we can move on."

Having someone call themselves a bitch kind of made it hard to call them a bitch. Or even think of them as a bitch, so much. Bailey thawed a tiny bit.

"How did you find out that Jane was hurt?"

Jeannie grimaced. "On the TV, likely the same as you. In spite of what Jane may have said, I don't always track her movements. Although, I admit, I have done so from time to time. But that jerk of a husband of hers made me paranoid."

Bailey looked off into the distance. "Yeah, I was watching Property Brothers and then next thing I knew I was waking up to the news - and there was Jane. I think I lost Olive before that, she zonked out earlier."

Jeannie eyed Olive speculatively. "Daship, eh? What nationality is that, Dutch?"

Olive swallowed. "Portuguese."

Jeannie nodded, then turned back to Bailey. "I've heard a lot about you, Ms. McCallum. Jane thinks very highly of you."

"Please, call me Bailey."

"Very well, Bailey. You may both call me Jeannie, if you wish."

There seemed to be nothing more to say at that point, so they all fell silent.

The waiting went on.

Along about 1am, a doctor came out. He looked harried, like doctors are supposed to look. He looked vaguely around the room, then asked for anyone here to speak for Cai Shun. Dai Shun stood, and the doctor stepped up to him and said, "Mister Shun is resting. It appears that he had a mild heart attack and he's doing quite well, all things considered."

Bailey spoke up, "May we see him yet, doctor?"

"We're allowing immediate family only, at this time. If the family wishes you to accompany them, that would be up to them." He spread his comments to the rest of the room. "Your visits must be very short. Mr. Shun is quite tired and will likely not be entirely conscious."

Dai Shun thanked the doctor and stood. "Ms. Bailey, Ms. Daship, would you care to go along with me to see Mr. Shun?"

Bailey and Olive nodded, and gratefully went with him to the nurse's station, where they were given a guide to take them into the Coronary Care Unit. They trailed the guide down the hallway until they came to a set of double doors, which he strode confidently though. A new hallway, much like the previous one, and then they turned into a doorway.

Lying on the bed, sprouting a multitude of wires and tubes, was Cai Shun. His eyes were open as they entered, and they brightened considerably on seeing visitors. His eyes darted around, and they looked disappointed. Bailey supposed he was trying to find Jane, so he may not be aware of how little time has passed. At any rate, he looked back at the little group, and his mouth twitched, likely his current approximation of a broad smile.

"Hey, Cai! Good to see you! That was quite a dive you made, good thing Jane was there to pull you up, huh?"

His eyes looked confused, then cleared a bit. His mouth twitched again.

"Jane's here at the hospital too, haven't heard much about her yet. We'll be here when she wakes, though. I'm sure she'll be raring to go soon, and you with her."

Dai said something in Chinese, and Cai remained impassive. Dai sighed and stepped back.

The attendant said, "Best you don't tire him. He needs to rest and relax those muscles so he can get better."

"Cai, you behave now. We'll take off and see you again soon."

Olive went over and gave him a gossamer kiss on his cheek, and winked.

He made the mouth twitch again. We backed out the door and waved as we went. The nurse took us back through the maze of corridors to the waiting room, where we resumed waiting.

Dai looked at us and said, "My father and I have not gotten along well in some years. We had a disagreement as to my choice of profession."

Bailey nodded in understanding. "That seems to be one of the top issues for disagreements among families. Cai's friend Jane has the same sort of issue with her mother." I rolled my eyes toward Jeannie, and he bowed slightly.

Olive and I sat there, a little desultory chat among the three sets of people sprouting up from time to time, then dying out.

After a while, Bailey rose and said, "I'm going to go find some coffee."

"I'll come along." This from Olive, who looked like she had the jitters bad enough that the last thing she needed was coffee.

They meandered down the hallway, following the requisite yellow line, (Cafeteria, 250 feet) and stepped through the doorway into the cafe. It was open and probably would look exactly the same in the daytime, considering it was located in the basement. It was just another institutional food location and apparently no one considered the cafeteria worthy of a window. Bailey grabbed a coffee to go, although to keep from worrying about someone yelling about theft, Olive waited to "have" hers until they sat at one of the many small tables.

"Can you actually taste that, Olive?"

Olive shrugged. "I don't have any baseline to tell me what it really tastes like, but I have a very good simulation of what it smells like turned into what I think it should taste like. Someday if I ever manage taste-buds, I'll probably be disappointed. One way or the other. At what I've been missing out on, or thanking the Maker that I didn't have to taste it before."

Bailey sat and sipped her coffee, as did Olive. They looked mostly at the walls and the institutional artworks hung to "brighten" the space. After a while it became just another waiting room, only with less comfortable seating, so they returned to the original waiting room. Finally, Bailey slumped over against the chair arm and Olive slumped over against her and they both slept. At least to outward appearances. Olive's processes stayed on full alert, just in case someone else should slide into the seat beside her and she'd need to "wake up" to ward them off.

Bailey slept fitfully, twitching and making odd little noises in her sleep. Olive watched her and her heart swelled, listening to the so very human person next to her. Bailey seemed to have it together normally, but right now, she seemed like an unhappy child in need of her mother.

Olive also watched Jane's mother. She became aware, over time, that Jeannie Bond was just as worried about Jane as they were. She tried to hide it, but in her own sleepless way, she was behaving much the same way as Bailey. The occasional tears and head bob told the story far more than anything she could have said, and Olive cataloged it all - resolving to possibly cut her some slack later on when she became the "army bitch" again.

Morning came. Everyone had slept in some way, none of them comfortable. Dai went to see his father again, but came back shortly.

Finally, after several days passing - that was really only 9am arriving - a doctor came out. He looked dead tired, but smiled at the waiting room in general. "Are there any of you who are here for Jane Bond?"

Nearly everyone in the waiting room sat up and paid attention, and he looked a little bemused at the differentiation between the groups.

"Jane is resting. She's still very much in danger, but barring complications, she'll pull through. She had extensive damage to her left lung and intestinal tract, but we were able to repair that, and she should recover just fine. One shattered rib we pieced back together and as long as she's careful in her movements it should be fine. As long as she rests. She is in very good health, and that contributes to her eventual recovery. She will need someone to be with her though. Will any of you be available to help her through the next several weeks while she works at becoming whole again?"

Three hands popped up immediately. Bailey, Olive and surprisingly enough to Bailey, Jeannie Bond.

The doctor nodded. "Very good. I must get back. You may visit her for very short amounts of time. We are requesting family and close friends only, at this point."

He turned and walked off into the never-never land of any large hospital.

Jeannie eyed Bailey and Olive. "I suppose we can all go, but if you excite her, I'll clear you out myself." To the silent ABU-dressed military minions sitting, she said, "Go back to base. I'll submit your new assignments, as it looks as if I'll be in Seattle or Chelan for a while." They nodded as one, rose as one and trooped off - as one. She smiled proudly after them, then turned toward the nurse's station and set off without further comment.

On arrival at the desk, she fastened her gimlet eye on the nearest nurse. "I'm Jeannie Bond, I'm here to see Jane Bond. I understand she's available for visitors. These are family friends who will be accompanying me. They should also be signed in as family friends to obviate interference at any future visits."

The nurse at the station seemed to be mesmerized by the woman and she simply took down Bailey and Olive's names, then called for a guide to take them to the ICU where Jane was being watched over.

The guide, this time a short dumpy female, took them through the maze of corridors, finally pointing them through a doorway. She followed them in and stood fairly unobtrusively against the wall.

The pitiful lump on the bed hardly looked like Jane. If anything, she had more tubes and wiring around her than Cai did. However, unlike Cai her eyes were open and while not much animation was there, she was definitely Jane.

A whisper from the bed. "Mother? Mother, what are you doing here? Oh, and Bailey - and Olive." She made an almost smile, but it was obviously something she had to struggle to do.

And then something very strange happened. Old battle axe Jeannie Bond, combat decorated, multiple campaigns, two-star general - she bent and kissed her daughter's forehead and decorated it with tears. "I love you, little one. I'm so glad you're ok." And then she stood back against the wall stiffly, motioning Bailey and Olive forward.

Blinking back tears at the sight, Bailey stroked Jane's cheek, "We were so worried about you, but you made it. You're a tough old bird."

Jane's eyebrows went up and she rasped, "Old bird? You're older than me!"

Bailey smiled and drew back, and Olive came forward, giving Jane one of her gossamer kisses. "You scared me so much, I'm not so sure being human is a good idea after all!"

Jane grinned, an almost Jane regular grin. "Being human is always a good idea, sweetie." Her voice faded out at the end though, and her eyes closed.

The nurse herded them back out of the room and pointed the right path to follow, and soon they were almost back to the waiting room.

Bailey said, "Um, let's all go into the cafeteria." She made the turn without seeing if they were following, but when she arrived at a table, Jeannie and Olive were there behind her. Bailey sat and Olive scrunched in beside her. Jeannie took the other side of the tiny table.

Impulsively, Bailey reached across the table and took Jeannie's hand. She found it cold - and trembling. "You're not exactly who I expected, Ms. Bond."

Jeannie looked at her a beat, then replied, "I'm not exactly who I was yesterday, Ms. McCallum."

Bailey looked around the room, then asked "Coffee?"

"Tea please, with two cream, two sugars."

Bailey chuckled. "If there was any doubt, that erased it. But do you expect everyone to follow your orders?"

"I do, Ms. McCallum, I most assuredly do."

Bailey shrugged expressively. "Then I guess I won't disappoint you. This time."

She came back shortly with her coffee, tea for Jeannie. She smirked at Olive. "You can get your own."

With a dramatic sigh, Olive went over to peruse the choices, coming back with something that looked like water but with bubbles. "Sprite."

"Have to be different, don't you?"

Olive smirked devilishly, "Yep."

Jeannie glanced around, then leaned in. "All right, what's really going on here?"

Bailey looked around as well, then also leaned forward and with her forehead nearly touching Jeannie's, she said, "Jane's hurt and in the hospital."

Jeannie's head snapped back as if she'd been slapped. "Ms. McCallum, I'd suggest you find a better tone and story. So many things can be made so much more inconvenient for you."

Fire came into Bailey's eyes and voice, "There's nothing you can do but wait - the same as I am, bitch. She may be your daughter, but she's been my best friend for years and she hasn't seen YOU much at all in that same number of years. Stand down or be rolled over."

This last came out in Bailey's patented boardroom hiss and it seemed to push back Jeannie Bond's attitude to nothing. Shockingly, she said, "I ... I'm sorry, Ms. McCallum. I'm ... she's my only child. And nearly 40 years of training doesn't just go away."

Bailey sat back and said, "My name is Bailey, Jeannie."

Jeannie Bond blinked, but said, "Very well ... Bailey."

"Anything that needs to be talked about can wait until Jane is here in person to discuss it. She's in charge of this little group, and we don't make a move without her." Which was patently a lie, but oddly truthful as well.

To her credit, Jeannie took it in stride, commenting only, "Do you have a place here in Seattle, Bailey, or should we acquire lodgings?"

"I have a small apartment not far from here, actually. It will be tight, but I doubt we'll be doing much sleeping anyhow, at least until Jane is out of the woods."

"What happened to her?"

"It's for Jane to decide what to say when she wakes. She's really the only one that can."

And Jeannie had to take that for an answer.

CHAPTER NINETEEN

The aftermath

They got back to the waiting room and there was a new arrival there. He was just about six feet tall, jeans and a button-down shirt. Boots on his feet, and a hat in his hand made him Dale. Bailey went over and gave him a big hug and he smiled and hugged her back.

"Just got in, how's she doin', Bailey."

"She's gonna make it, Dale. She's hurting pretty bad, though."

He looked around the room, then drew Bailey off to one side and bent toward her. In a low voice, "She was your best friend, did she talk to you about anything ... um ..."

Bailey smiled slightly at him. "Not until just a few weeks ago, but I know what you're saying - about the strange stuff."

Dale blew out a gusty sigh, "I thought this was over with - that Kit was gone, and she'd be free of getting into dangerous messes. What happened to that happy idea?"

"It's complicated. And not something we can talk about here. Jane's mother is here, for one thing."

"Oh, great, that should make Jane happy."

"Yeah. I had to put the bitch in her place already this morning."

Dale's eyebrows went up. "How the hell did you manage that?"

Grimly, "I've lived in a shark tank for years ... but also, I think she's hurting more than I would have expected."

Bailey pulled him back over to where Jeannie and Olive were still waiting, staring at the new arrival. "Guys, this is Dale McDaniels. Dale, this is Olive Daship and Jeannie Bond."

Jeannie appraised him and nodded. "Good to meet you, mister McDaniels."

"Likewise, Ms. Bond. Is Mister Bond here as well?"

"No, not yet, Joe is stuck trying to find transport. He should be here shortly, however, I believe he flew into JBLM not long ago. He'll be here when he can get transportation."

"If you'll pardon me, ma'am, what's JBLM?"

"Oh. Joint Base Lewis-McChord. It's the airlift base near Tacoma."

He nodded in understanding. "Ok."

He turned to Olive. "And you, ma'am?"

Olive grinned. "I'm Olive, I'm the sidekick."

Dale chuckled. "That make you Robin or Jimmy Olson?"

Olive flexed a hand at him, her fingers in claws. "I'm more Catwoman." She smirked a patented Olive smirk that she'd no doubt been practicing in the 'mirror'. "I've heard all about you, buddy."

Dale raised an eyebrow. "Should I feel honored or threatened?"

Olive, again with the smirk, "Yes."

He grinned. "Ok, so should I go see Jane or let her alone?"

Jeannie spoke up, "It took us about five minutes to tire her out and she looked like she was sleeping when we left not more than ten minutes ago. Perhaps you should let her rest."

Dale frowned, but said, "Ok, I guess."

Bailey put a hand on his shoulder. "She's probably right, but Jane was conscious enough to make a sarcastic remark at me, so I think she's gonna be ok. Maybe wait a couple hours and we'll all go invade her space."

Dale shrugged. "Ok. Y'all got rigs to drive?"

"Olive's got her smartcar here, but it's only big enough for about one and a half people, so maybe we can take your truck?"

He barked a laugh. "I guess you do know Jane, if you know I gotta have a truck no matter where I go. Yeah, I got a four-door Jimmy out in the lot. We can all take it - what, to IHOP? I looked it up, it ain't too far."

Olive spoke up, "I'll drive my own car. We'll probably want t' settle in at Bailey's 'partment afore we come back here, too. It don' sound like we'll be leavin for a few days."

"Ok, we'll meet you at IHOP, then."

They split off, Olive heading over to where she'd left the ship, and the others following Dale to his truck.

At IHOP, where mysteriously Olive arrived first and had a table before the others got there, they sat and ate. After the long stressful night, they were all starved and were fairly silent until the food was delivered. Then they started eating. They each shared a story or two about Jane, and that made them all people to each other, their commonality - Jane.

Food gone and all of them stuffed, they met at Bailey's apartment. Thank goodness it was a ground floor flat with a garage, otherwise they might have had to make up a story about why Olive couldn't join them. It was difficult anyhow in such close quarters, but at least as long as Jeannie was there, Olive's secret had to stay deep and dark.

It was a small two-bedroom apartment. Bailey and Olive would share Bailey's room, Jeannie would take the guest room and poor Dale was relegated to the couch. At least it was a large comfortable couch. Of course, Dale wound up spending most of this time at the hospital anyhow, sitting by Jane's bed, hour after hour.

Jeannie got a call, and came back looking a combination of devastated and steamed. "That was Joe. He stopped in at the hospital, saw Jane - who was asleep - and then ... and then he left. He flew back out of JBLM just a few minutes ago."

Since no one in the room was quite able to come up with something to say, no one said anything. But Bailey hugged her hard. Maybe that was enough.

CHAPTER TWENTY

Recovery

I woke up hurting all over and barely able to open my eyes. I realized that my mother was bent over and staring at me.

"Mother? Mother, what are you doing here?"

I looked a little past her and saw, to my relief, Bailey. And thank goodness, Olive.

"Oh, and Bailey. And Olive!" I tried to smile but it just hurt too much."

And then it was just weird. My mom, cranky grump that she is, bent down and actually kissed my forehead. She said, "I love you, little one. I'm so glad you're ok." I don't remember that happening since I was just a little kid. I must be in bad shape for her to be that emotional.

And then Bailey, trying not to cry, put out her hand to touch my cheek. "We were so worried about you, but you made it. You're a tough old bird."

I tried to laugh, but something stabbed me in the chest and I just managed to whisper, "Old bird? You're older than me!"

And then Olive. She kissed me on the cheek, but I couldn't feel anything, so she must be pushed to her limit here. "You scared me so much, I'm not sure being human is a good idea after all!"

That made me smile, even through the pain and numbness. "Being human is always a good idea, sweetie." I could feel myself drifting though, even as I was talking.

I remember jumbled up dreams, the unearthly metal, the crater wall, Dale ... Dale ...

"Dale? Dale??"

And out of the darkness beside the bed, his deep voice saying, "I'm here, Jane."

I slipped back in it again, but this time the dreams weren't nightmares, and Dale was in all of them.

"..think she can hear us when she's asleep? I've always wondered ab ... Hey, Jane!"

I was feeling a little vague, but at least ALL of me didn't hurt now.

"I can hear you just fine, but only when I've been woken up by loud people!" It still came out in a whispery rasp, but I felt like I could talk.

Bailey came into view and I realized she and Olive were both there, with mother and Dale hanging in the background.

"Hey, you all don't have better things to do than wake up a sick woman?"

General laughter, then, "This IS what we do, Jane. We travel around the hospital now and wake people up so they can take their sleeping pills."

I said, more seriously, "Hey ... um ... how am I doing? What's wrong with me?"

Bailey and Olive exchanged looks and Bailey said, "Looks like some kind of fishing accident, Jane. Maybe a harpoon or something went through your side, messed up stuff pretty bad inside and smashed a rib on the way out. Olive and I were in Chelan, Cai was with you. I guess you must have decided to show him how to fish or something. Anyway, he had on a wetsuit and wound up with a heart attack. No one seems to know how it happened. And no one found the harpoon."

I took this in kind of vaguely, thinking there was something important I was missing, then nodded. "Harpoon, huh. No wonder it hurt so much."

"You're healing fast - a lot faster than they expected, for some reason. Must be all that working out and healthy living, huh?"

I was feeling a little vague again, but not enough to pass out yet. "Yeah, that must be it. All that working out paid off. Also the vodka sours and the screwdrivers."

Olive spoke up, looking a little concerned. "Your eyes looked weird at first, Jane. Are you seeing okay now?"

I frowned, barely remembering that I'd probably been in vacuum for a while. "Yes, I'm seeing fine." I looked around the room, finally registering that I hadn't seen Cai. "Cai? Are you here?"

Bailey took a breath, "He's here in the hospital too, Jane. He had a heart attack, but he's on the mend and he'll probably be out before you. We think you must have gotten him up from a deep dive and that's why your eyes looked odd - like you were depressurized too fast."

I nodded. I could see I'd have to be careful to stick with the story they were telling me. At least I hadn't seen any police, so it didn't seem to be a problem with that. "Yeah, I don't really remember much though, to tell you the truth." Which was pretty close to the real truth.

"You lost a lot of blood, honey. It was pretty bad, in fact, that seems to be more the issue at this point, your system has a lot of catching up to do. Do you remember anything about someone putting a bandage on you?" She was slowly shaking her head.

"No, Bailey, to be honest I don't remember much about that day at all. It seems like it was years ago, like it's all fuzzy with time. It's not been that long, has it?"

"No, it's only been a couple days, Jane."

Dale elbowed his way back up to the front, and smiled at me. "Hey, you need some help, ma'am?"

Tears came unbidden to my eyes and I said, "All I can get, mister." I made kissy face at him and he kissed me. I must taste gross, my mouth feels really ikky. "You don't have to kiss the sicky, sicky." But I smiled at him. A lot. "Where are we? In Chelan?"

Bailey smirked, "No, of course not, Jane. How could you be in Chelan. You're at Harborview Medical in Seattle. It's the one with the great ... harbor ... view."

I tried to shrug and made a mess of it. "Well, like I say, it seems like years ago. When can I go home?"

From Dale, "Soon, baby, soon." He smiled so warmly at me it made me tingle. I started to drift again then, they must be giving me some great drugs.

I woke up and looked around a little. I could hear a funny noise over to the side and I managed to look over there. Dale was sitting, snoring softly in his chair. The sun was coming in the blinds and I felt pretty good. I tried moving my hands and that seemed to work. I moved my head some more and looked around the room. Seemed whoever was in this room was pretty popular. I even saw a big poster-painted card signed with a lot of very sloppy names and a big "Chelan Elementary School" painted on the side, and on the other side "Get Well Ms. Bond!" It was really cute, all flowery and looked like a lot of kids had worked on it. Flowers, balloons and lots of cards. Wow. Even a plant. I had to giggle, it was a prickly pear cactus in bloom. I won't do that again, giggling hurts. A lot.

As long as I didn't laugh, or do anything like breathe, I was fine. I lay there just looking at all the stuff around me. Life is pretty good, and trust me, it's a hell of a lot better than the alternative. I've been too close to that a few times and it's not for me. At least not without a fight. I started taking stock of my parts. I could move my hands, my feet, I could only twitch my legs a little but that was probably only 'cause they were under the blankets. For all I know, I'm strapped down. As far as I could tell, no paralysis of anything. Which was good. I was just doing eyebrow exercises when Dale woke up.

"Hey there, beautiful!"

"Who are YOU talking to, mister?"

"Who do you think, Miss?"

I peered around theatrically, "There must be a nurse in here who I can't see."

He came closer, leaned over and kissed me. "No, it's you. It's always you."

I smiled and said, "So, when are you busting me out of here? I wanna go home."

"Probably pretty soon, they seem to think you're healing really well. No infection at all, for some reason, and that really helped the healing speed. You'll have a lot of pain, but that will be pretty much the same here or at home. If you want to go home, I'll push them harder."

"Oh, I definitely want to go home."

He smiled and looked fabulous. "Then I'll push them harder, starting right now." One more kiss and he walked out of the room.

I lay back and in spite of my brave words, I almost immediately fell back asleep.

Next time I woke up, Dale was back in his chair again, asleep again. I must have been out for a while. I felt a lot more wide awake this time, and I found out later they'd cut back my pain meds and drugs. I'd have to start eating and the like on my own. Which sounds like a good thing, right? Well, maybe not so much. Turns out one reason I've been feeling pretty good is that I was pumped full of pain meds and when that started wearing off, I started hurting - a lot. I considered begging to go back on my drugs, but then I thought about my sunny little corner of the world and decided maybe I'd suck it up and not whine. Much. I did whine enough to get some Percoset, and apparently I'm pretty susceptible to it 'cause later I got some really weird dreams. The docs had said I could leave tomorrow, but I have no idea what tomorrow is at this point. I'll ask Dale when he wakes up, or when someone else gets here.

It was quite a kick being loaded into an air-ambulance and being whisked away. The trip was by no means as fast or smooth as riding with Olive, but it was dang close. They were able to land in the field over the garage and they rolled me down right into my living room. After checking me out to make sure nothing had come loose in the flight, they left. Dale had flown with me, and I expected Olive and Bailey to turn up soon. And no doubt my mother would arrive, somewhat put out to be last, no doubt. Bailey said that she had been very human while I was mostly dead, and I was looking forward to trying to see if she'd changed, or it was just temporary fright of nearly losing her only daughter.

As expected, Bailey and Olive walked through the door from the downstairs conference room not very much later. I wasn't sure that Dale knew anything about it, and from his reaction - first surprise, then irritation, then resignation - he hadn't known much.

He eyed Bailey and Olive, then turned to me. "It's not over, is it?"

I shook my head gently. "No, it's not. It never really was. We had a wonderful vacation, but I'm sure we'll have to return to saving the world."

I raised my arm in greeting, and even that little movement hurt. This being damaged sucks, I'm looking forward to being past that! "Hi guys. Have a nice flight?"

I watched Dale, worried about his attitude, but he'd known what he was buying when he got me and I thought he'd come around ok.

"Dale? Are you ok, honey?"

He looked at me for a long moment, then nodded his head. "Yeah, this is what I signed on for, I guess. You can't keep from laying your life on the line and I guess that's one of the things I loved about you."

He kissed me. I could hear both Bailey and Olive sighing, whether it was disgust over the PDA, or relief over him saying that, I wasn't sure.

"Olive?"

"Yes, boss."

"Show Dale ... your ... tricks."

She grinned. "Which ones, I got a lot of 'em."

"Well, first off, let him try to shake your hand."

Dale looked at me oddly, then reached out for Olive's hand. She put it out willingly and his hand went right through it. He recoiled like it was a snake, and his eyes got big.

Gently, I said, "Dale, she's like Kit. Only she's got more power than he did, and she can project an image of herself. Did you notice that she never got close to anyone when you were at the hospital in Seattle? It was because she had to be very careful not to let anyone know she doesn't have a real body, and she has to be within a certain distance of her ship - which you've seen as the little smartcar - to even be able to make that projection."

"Olive, can you shake hands with Dale, please?"

She smiled and said, "Yassuh, boss."

She stuck out her paw and Dale, looking confused, put out his hand, expecting to find empty air again. He was doubly confused when he found a warm, seemingly human hand. This time he let go of it slowly, seeming to be almost in awe.

"She can generate actual physical parts when she's here in the house. The main computer is downstairs in the big room where we spent so much time, and it's much more powerful than the one in the ship. She's limited in how much she can do, and right now is limited to hands and the like."

"Right now?"

"Yes. Right now. She's working at doing more."

"I ... see."

"We've had that discussion and we're comfortable with her not becoming Hal, so don't worry about that. We'll go into more detail later, but I wanted to cover what needed to be covered before my mother gets here. She knows nothing about any part of this life."

"Olive, can you take Dale on a quick ride in the ship? Just a short one, so he knows what it can do. Bailey, bring me some chips, please?" I made my best invalid face at her and she rolled her eyes.

"Did the doctors say you can have that?"

"Nope. But they didn't say I couldn't and I'm not looking at my diet requirements until I get my chips and salsa."

"Bossy cow."

I smiled at her and leaned back, watching Dale and Olive disappear into the house.

Bailey reappeared with the chips, salsa and some various things to drink.

"I brought you water and PepsiMax just in case. I'm serious about the diet, honey. We really need to make sure you don't do anything to anything."

I sighed. "It was my lung, not my stomach."

"It took out a chunk of your intestine, too!"

"Oh. Well, yeah. I kinda forgot about that." I looked at the bowl of chips, the salsa, the drinks. I frowned. "I'll have water I guess." And then, morosely, "And some of that yellow baby food they sent along, I suppose."

I started eating the "Apples and Fruit!", which was kinda weird, considering that apples are already fruit, aren't they? At any rate, it tasted like some kind of sugary paste made of flavoring and vitamin pills. I looked sadly at the chips that Bailey was chowing down on, but I behaved.

Olive and Dale came back and since he was only pale, not puking, I figured that keeping the trip short had saved him. I grinned at him and offered him some "Apples and Fruit!" but he declined. He seemed to like the chips too. Everyone friggin liked the chips.

I finally gagged down my "Apples and Fruit!" and said, "We need to talk about what happened and what we need for plans. Obviously, there's more now that we don't know about. Olive, can you tell us what happened?"

Olive looked at her hands, then said, "I can show you. It might be easier than telling you. But it won't be pretty, and you all should be sitting. Maybe with a bowl nearby."

I said, "Oh, that bad, huh?"

Olive nodded. "Yeah, that bad."

A hole seemed to open in front of us, a hole we could see the moon through. It was a perfect shot of the surface, and you could see the Chinese expedition cameras. There was some desultory conversation and after a while (sped up, Olive mentioned) the cameras nosed down. After a back and forth of conversation that I didn't remember a bit of, three people filed into the picture and made their way across the screen to the far side of the crater wall. The camera followed them, seeming to have been run by an expert cameraman. Then, I could see all of us close to the artifact. A bit of hesitation, then I reached out and grabbed the thing. The action slowed down to a crawl and I could see as I touched it, the skinsuit seemed to dissolve away from where it had touched the alien metal, and especially taking the speed of the video into account, the suit must have seemed to vanish.

Olive said, "Jane, you might want to close your eyes here."

Like a fool, I ignored her. The film started again, and the item showed itself to be a piece of the alien glass metal about a foot long and half an inch in diameter. It moved. It moved, seemed to aim itself and simply shot away from the crater. I was bent over, the suit mostly gone with just a bit remaining on the far side of my body. The "thing" launched. It went straight away from where it was embedded, and I happened to be standing in front of it. I could see it enter my lower abdomen, and then practically instantaneously it shot out of my upper left side, having punched through anything in the way. Blood and tissue exploded in a fog behind me. I could see a look of shock come over my face that probably mirrored what was on my face now. My body fell to the ground and blood began exiting in great gouts. Cai shrieked, a scream that must have damaged his throat. I could see him attempting to cover the wound with his hand while scooping me up. I could see him hitting the side of the crater with me dangling from his arms, a bloody trail left behind us. The ship with its wide-open door intersected his bounce off the crater wall and Cai fell through the door, dropping me on the floor. He seemed to crumple to the floor and lie still. Olive showed how human she'd become by dithering about for a few seconds, then grabbed a bandage from somewhere and pasted it over my gushing wound. Immediately the blood stopped flowing. I realized the ship was already moving and had been while she was attempting first aid. It took no longer than a few minutes and I'm not sure that Olive even sped up the video. The door popped open and Olive screamed at Cai to "get Jane out of the ship". Cai lay still. Olive, tears flowing freely, started pulling on me, her hands slipping in the gore, but managing to get me down the ramp. Then she returned to the ship, and about all there was of Olive at that point WAS hands. She managed to get Cai dumped off the bottom, then the camera view moved away. There was no longer any sign of Olive. She was simply gone.

The room was in utter silence. I was regretting with every fiber of my being having watched the presentation. From the look around the room, everyone was feeling the same.

We all sat, stunned. After a few minutes, people began to come to life again, albeit more like zombies than regular people. After milling about aimlessly for a while, someone thought to turn on the TV. A mindless sitcom came on and we watched, soaking up the stupid until we began to find a way to live with life again. After an hour or two, we were some semblance of normal and it was well, since shortly after that I heard tires on the gravel driveway. Mother had managed to catch a flight out of Seattle, landing in Wenatchee, I guess. I would have giggled when I saw the car, but it would have hurt too much. For someone used to driving (or being driven in) a large HumVee, driving a tiny Kia herself must have been excruciating.

Her eyebrows went up seeing Bailey and Olive already there, but she seemed to be trying to take it all in stride. I had no doubt there would be repercussions though.

And dammit, she liked the chips and salsa too. By then, everyone was more or less over the shakes and had been making inroads in the food again. I suppose that's why there's always so much food at funerals. Somehow eating validates life.

I decided I'd go to bed. I was a little scared to stand, but with Mother on one side and Dale on the other I managed to stand and even shuffle carefully to the couch. I'd decided taking the stairs might be too much to ask, and I think that was wise, since I was pretty woozy and hurting after just the trip to the couch. I fell asleep almost instantly, distantly aware of the murmur of chat between all four of my keepers. I had no dreams that I remember, for that I was grateful.

I woke in the morning, heard pots and pans being moved around in the kitchen and jumped up to remind Olive that she needed to be all there if she was going to make pancakes. That is, I started to jump up and was forcibly reminded that I don't jump up right now. I made some sort of pathetic eeep noise and lay back down, my side and ribs screaming at me. The pan rattling noises stopped, and my mother came in.

She looked worried, said, "Are you all right? I heard something that sounded like a muffled scream."

"I just tried to jump up - I forgot I can't do that right now. Of course, now I'm really hurting. Can you get me a pain pill, mother? I think I left them outside."

Softly, "I brought them in last night, I left them and a glass of water on the table - here." She pointed right in front of me.

"I said, "Doh. Now I feel like an idiot."

She smiled and said, "You have a lot of allowance for idiot right now, dear."

"Thanks ... mom."

"I checked your diet plan. It seems to me that pancakes qualify for 'soft food' at least as much as 'Apples and Fruit!' do. So, I thought I'd make pancakes. I'm sorry I woke you hunting for pans, though."

"Mother, since when do you make pancakes?"

She crossed her arms and looked at me. "I suppose I deserve anything you heap on me. I was a lousy mom. But I used to make pancakes, back when Joe and I were just starting out and we had time." She sounded wistful, like she was caressing a memory. "I'm far enough up the ladder now that I have some time again, but by now Joe and I aren't that close either. And you hate me."

"Oh geez, mom. I don't hate you. I just don't know you."

"Well, I'm making pancakes. And I'm going to try to get to know you better. It was such a shock - I really thought I was going to lose you. And it - it woke me up, Jane. Like nothing ever has."

I didn't quite know what to do with this information. I'd thought of my mother as cold and distant for so long it was hard to wrap my mind around anything else. And besides, making pancakes once hardly makes up for years of being invisible.

"Well, pancakes sounds really good, mom. But you might hold off until everyone ..." About then, Bailey came down the stairs with Olive trotting behind. Dale materialized out of the woodwork, he must have been in my bed. Which means - mom must have been here with me all night, since Dale would have been here otherwise.

"Mom, did you spend the night in the recliner?"

She looked at me, "Well, I certainly wasn't going to leave you alone here." She laughed, which - trust me - was also weird, and said, "Dale and I arm wrestled for it, but I won."

"Am I in the Twilight Zone here?"

"Mmhmm, we're all pod people, waiting for you to sleep again." This from Olive, with a maniac grin and eye rolling.

I waved my hands at all of them. "Get outta here, I gotta go pee!"

Bailey muttered, "Well, get up from the couch first 'cause I'm not cleaning it!"

I gasped, "Bailey, I thought you were my friend! I'd clean up pee for you!"

She just rolled her eyes expressively and they all left me alone. Well, that's not true, Dale pretended to leave, but he came back and helped me up, then helped me to the bathroom, then offered to come help IN the bathroom, which I drew the line at. And regretted. You use a lot of muscles getting up and down from the toilet. I had to beg in a tiny voice for him to come help me back up again. It just hurt too much.

He got me up and we made the long trip to the kitchen, where I finally got to sit in my favorite breakfast nook. Mom's pancakes were pretty good, although she didn't have any fancy moves like juggling the turner.

We sat and talked a bit, then Dale said, "Huh. That's interesting. Wasn't it the Carderas mine you were interested in, Jane?"

I said, "Yeah. It was an old gold mine we were looking for." I'd never really gone into much detail about the mine, the digging and the mountain lion. I figured what Dale didn't know wouldn't hurt me.

"Well, it looks like there was some kind of localized earthquake there the same night you were hurt. I just never saw the news item until now. I don't know the area that well, but it sounds like the right place. Heck of a thing, there was a forest fire and all. I guess they're still mopping up the mess now. The side of the mountain is just pretty well gone from the pictures."

He passed me his phone and I felt a cold chill. The area where the mine entered the mountain was simply gone. There was a huge black hole there. I wordlessly showed it to Olive, and she pulled out her own phone and started looking at it. I handed Dale his phone back and we all sat there, thinking.

My mother finally stood, looking annoyed. "Do you all really think I'm this stupid? I'll leave the room so you can talk about whatever this means to you. But I know there's something important going on that you're not telling me. And I understand it. But you can't keep it secret forever." And with that, she marched out to the deck, where she sat looking out over the water.

"Whoof. She's right, and her being here, we're going to have to either send her away or tell her something sooner or later. But for the time being, Olive, can you and Bailey go take a look at the mountain? And scan it, of course."

Olive nodded. "We're on our way." Bailey grabbed her drink and they headed downstairs to the garage.

Dale helped me up and we went outside. We wordlessly sat on the loungers next to mother. She was cold at first, but seemed to give it up and we wound up chatting about whatever innocuous things we could. After what seemed like an eternity, I heard Bailey and Olive come back into the kitchen.

Dale did his helper routine and got me back on my feet and I headed back into the house, flashing mother an "I'm sorry." as I passed her. She looked angry, and turned toward the water.

I sat down in my nook again and waited for them to fill us in. It wasn't going to be happy. Bailey looked grim, and there was no humor in Olive's eyes at all.

"The mountain is gone, the artifacts are gone. We'd decided it was the armaments controls and the hydroponics, which we really didn't care about. But the hydroponics section had a lot of spare power available as it had to be autonomous if anything happened to the ship. With no humans on board, it just was ignored. But it was kept fully at the ready."

"It has guns, Jane. Whatever it is has power and guns."

Coming in 2019 or 2020 – an excerpt from Lacey & Alex and the Dagger of Ill Repute.

LACEY & ALEX EXCERPT

Dying to get out.

Alex and I walked along the sidewalk toward the Fairmont, but part way there, I said, "Y'know, it's probably pointless to walk to the Fairmont when we don't have any idea who it is we're really looking for. Maybe we should make a run to the morgue and see if they have an ID on the body yet."

I looked at Alex to see what her reaction was. Oddly enough, there wasn't one. The morgue isn't usually high on the list of places people go to visit. At least, under their own power. I continued, "I'm not gonna walk there, though. I guess we can use some of her money to go visit her."

And Alex shrugged. So maybe she was listening.

There were quite a few floating cabs around the area so we grabbed one and had her take us to the morgue. The new SF Medical Examiner's office is pretty snazzy. It's even got a sculpture outside, but I doubt even the artist could tell you what it is. I have to admit though, I kinda like it. The building is all glass and metal and modern looking. Maybe they're trying to make up for what's always inside, no matter what the outside looks like. Of course, having a gothic nightmare of a Medical Examiner's office might be unpopular in the neighborhood.

We walked in the big airy front office and I stopped at the reception desk. I smiled politely and asked for Renny Montgomery. She asked for my name and I gave it, then she dialed her phone and turned away. A bit later she turned back to me and smiled a more real smile. "Renny will be with you in a moment." Renny may not have a fancy title, but she effectively runs the place. We had a "thing" awhile back, and I was hoping she remembered the good parts and not the bad.

She came out through the elevator door wearing a perfectly tailored grey Anne Klein business suit with an elegant pencil skirt and black high heels. I guess her memory was of the good parts, since she smiled and came over and hugged me.

"It's been too long, Lace. How have you been?"

We chatted at pleasantries for a bit, me ignoring the glances at Alex. Finally though, I took pity on her and said, "This is Alex, she's a friend. A straight friend, unfortunately." I grinned at Alex and then at Renny. Renny nodded, Alex looked at me blankly, the visual equivalent of a shrug, I guess.

Renny hauled us back through the new building, pointing out various and sundry bits as we talked. It was obvious she was proud of where she worked. And rightly so, the old building had been a dungeon. Almost literally. We got to her office, which was a nice little place, well lighted, although no window. I remarked on that and Renny smirked and said "It'll come, it'll come."

Once we were safely in her office, I told Renny what I needed, and she frowned, "I can't really release any details to the public, you know that, Lacey."

"Yea, I know, but the name is gonna be in the paper tomorrow anyhow, right? Or even tonight depending on when they go to press. This was downtown, it's gonna get some coverage. Hell, there were even TV trucks there."

She looked at me a moment, finally said, "Well, ok. But if anything happens, it didn't come from me. Just the name?"

I agreed and she tappity tapped at the computer for a bit and finally said, "Well, she came in as a Jane Doe, but looks like they must have found some ID on her someplace." Her eyebrows went up. "Wow, she's a heavy hitter. Ever hear of Evelyn Weintraub?"

I drew a blank. "No, not that I can think of. Who is she?"

"Well, she's the owner of Phillips and Potts, for one thing. Or she was. I guess she's not anymore."

I hazarded a guess. "The department store chain?"

She nodded. "The very same. Nice place, I guess you don't shop there." She grinned at me. She was always a slave to fashion, and I was always a slave to whatever was cheap. One of the many reasons we're not still together.

"No, I don't shop there. You always looked perfect though."

"Same old Lace - always with the compliments."

I looked at her soberly. "Always meant it, too."

She smiled. "I know. That's why I saw you today. Don't be a stranger, Lace."

I nodded. "I'll work on it."

Renny led us out to the reception area again - it's a good thing, since I'd have been lost. Maybe I could have asked the plants along the way, though, and gotten Alex to translate. We hit the sidewalk and I could feel her looking at me. Finally I said, "What?"

She shrugged. I shrugged. "Irreconcilable differences."

We pulled up in front of my apartment building, hopped out of the taxi, and went in. As we got near the door, I could hear the phone ringing inside. I managed to get the door open and dashed in to grab the phone. "Hello?"

Renny's voice, "Hey. I see you never did get a real phone."

Slightly wounded. "This IS a real phone. I just hate having a leash."

I could hear the grin in her voice, "Not always. But, this isn't about that. You still short a TV?"

"Uh huh. Can't see the point in that either."

"Well, if you had a TV you could turn on channel 24 and look at the party going on downtown. It's a great party, lots of celebrities, local personages, political hacks, Evelyn Weintraub ... "

I blinked. "I thought you had Evelyn Weintraub on a slab."

"I do. Or at least I have someone that looks just like the Evelyn Weintraub that's walking around the stage downtown right now."

"What, twins or something?"

"Not according to the internet, which you could also look up if you had a computer. Can I call you a luddite yet? Anyhow, she's supposedly an only child. And her mom's sister doesn't have any other kids anywhere close to that age. And if they were, both of them are boys to boot.

I just stood there in silence for a minute. "Ok, thanks for letting me know, Ren. Are you planning on doing anything about it?"

"Well, we're notifying next of kin right now. But, all things considered, I'm not sure what to do. I mean, she looks very much alive. It's going to be a bit of a shock for someone - like her - to come in here and see herself. Dead." She sighed. "I'll let the bosses know, let them handle it. This is why it's nice NOT to be the M.E. Assuming Evelyn comes in, I'll swab some DNA for comparison. If she doesn't, I suppose I'll have to send someone out to track her down and do it. Honestly though, I feel like I should hear the "Twilight Zone" music in the background."

I nodded, as if she could hear my head rattle, thanked her, and hung up.

I looked at Alex.

She said, "Evelyn Weintraub is alive?"

I shook my head in puzzlement. "Yes and no. Apparently the body is resting comfortably at 1 Newhall, but Evelyn is at a party right now and she's pretty active for a dead person.

COMING IN 2019 OR 2020 – AN EXCERPT FROM CINNAMON ROLL CAPERS – CATNAPPED

I managed to get under him and got his shoulders, picked him up and cradled his head between my breasts. At least they have SOME use. I dragged him outside, down the two steps trying to bang him around as little as possible.

I managed to get my butt over the passenger seat and levered him up and in the Jeep, then slithered out from under him and out the driver side. Back around to the other side, I got his legs up and inside the footwell, then arranged him and buckled him in. I got an old blanket out of the back and tried to get his head padded so it wouldn't move from side to side much. Crap. This is gonna be bad.

I slammed the door shut on the house, and the passenger side of the Jeep, then jumped in the driver side. I cranked her up, and backed off the lawn, whipped around and started off down the mountain. I tried to minimize the side to side motion, but it was tough. I decided it might be better to take it slow rather than beat him deader or run off the edge of a cliff, and it took me nearly 30 minutes to get him back to town. I arrived unceremoniously at the little clinic and ran inside, reporting what I had. A couple people grabbed a gurney and I left it to them at that point, getting him out and inside. I talked to the receptionist and hung around for a bit, then went out and moved Anna-the-Jeep to the parking lot.

I called Mary and told her what happened, and she started laughing. "Yeah, I bet. It's a great joke, but I'm not buying."

I said, "This is no joke. I'm here at the clinic, the mayor is inside with a bloody head. I'm not even sure if he's gonna make it, he was out completely when I got to his house."

Dead silence. Then, "This isn't some kind of revenge for the cat thing, right? I mean, I just wanted you to meet him."

Slow burn. "You mean, it really WAS a setup? There was no catnapping or anything?"

"Uh, no. Catnapping, for 50k? Are you kidding?"

Shouting now, "Then why was he knocked out with a bloody head wound in the entrance of his house?? You better get over here NOW, Mare." One thing I miss about landline phones was the ability to slam the handset down, it's not anywhere near as satisfying to click that little button, no matter how hard you push it.

Two minutes later, I heard a siren start up across town and a little over five minutes later, she was parked in the lot next to me. After telling me, "If this is a joke, I'll have your skin!" she dashed inside.

Now that it wasn't my problem anymore, I walked inside more sedately and asked the nearest blue coated person if they knew any more about Mayor Paul's condition, but no one was willing to say anything. I sat down in the waiting room and did just that. I called the shop and made sure we were covered and got a report. It had been a fairly slow morning, but Gina had taken care of things for me, then Franny had come in at the usual time. I told them a tiny bit about what had happened and let them know I'd be in later, hopefully in time for noon rush.

Pretty soon, Mary came out to the waiting room and sat down beside me. She asked, "Um, are I dead?"

I patted my sister's hand and said, "No, but I definitely owe you one. Or you owe me one. Either way, it's big."

She sighed and nodded. "I know."

"Now, give."

"Not a lot to give. I thought you should meet him, he's rich and single and about your age. You have a lot in common, but he's not the kind of guy you'd probably meet at the bakery and he's got his own gym." She shrugged helplessly. "I just thought, if you had a reason to go up there then - you would both get a good laugh over it and maybe do coffee or something. He's a nice guy, really."

I said, "Well, as it turns out, it's a good thing you decided to do your little trick - otherwise he might have laid there for quite a while before anyone thought to check up on him."

A smile broke out on her sad face, "Oh, that's true!"

I smiled and hugged her. "See, always a silver lining."

She laughed. "That's my line, Cin." She sobered instantly though, "He's in bad shape, but it looks like he'll probably make it. From the way the blood is dried and matted into his hair, he probably laid like that for a while. I sent Doris up to look at his place, see if she can find anything." She looked back at me, "Cin, can you look at this one? I mean, we have very little experience with something like this. I'll talk to the town council, but I doubt we'll have a problem covering your expenses at your shop if you have to take time off."

I sighed and said, "Yea, I'll look at it, Mare. If you think Mitchell can't handle it. She might surprise you, though. She seems damn competent."

"I know. I'll talk with her when she gets back, but there is the thing about timing too. I'll call Seth back from vacation if I have to, but that'll be tough on him and his family. It's a small town, Cin, but it's not that small."

"Ok, just let me know. I called in to the bakery, they should be ok for now, but I want to head over there by 11:30 or so. Good thing I left early this morning."

"Um ... along that line, Cinny ... "

"What? Why do I have the feeling I'm being railroaded someplace?"

Mary tried to look innocent. "Maybe it's the gentle sound of the train whistle?"

I rolled my eyes. "Ok, out with it. What is it that you want me to tease out of you?"

"It's not really that. See - you know Rose over at Brew and Bagel?"

"Uh huh, I get bagels there sometimes."

"Well, she's going to have to close. She's run the numbers and she won't be able to survive another winter."

I sighed. "It's so awful when someone loses their dream, and she made such great bagels. And coffee, for that matter."

"Mmmhmm ... sure will be sad losing the best coffee and the only bagel place in town. And Rose is such a peach, always there to help when you need her. It was her dream to own a coffee shop, she's been saving for years."

I finally began to get an inkling where this was going. "So, gonna pour on some more honey to cover the BS, or just hand it to me straight?"

Mary looked me up and down. "Well, remember how you've commented that you really wish you had allocated a bit more space for another apartment instead of so much space for the bakery?"

"Maaaybe ... why?" I was determined to make her drag this out of me.

"Oh for Lord's sake, Cin, if Rose moved into The Cinnamon Roll with you, you'd have coffee and bagels to sell along with the pastries - and everyone knows that coffee goes perfect with donuts, right?"

"Well, yea, but it goes perfect with bagels too, and that means they'd buy less donuts and cut into my income."

"But if the overall income was higher since people'd be coming to buy coffee instead of just rolls, it would be better. AND she can help share the cost of the building with you, which decreases your overhead. She helps pay down your mortgage, stays in business and saves her dream, and is there at the same time of the morning as YOU are, just in case ... "

I sighed. "Just in case - what?"

Mary rolled her eyes. "Just in case you're gone out on a case, ditz."

"Hah! I got you to admit it. You're trying to poach a new cop!"

She shrugged. "That was pretty damned obvious. But this way, I get a part time cop that I can call for help when I need it, without having to justify a full-time officer. And you have such great credentials - remember what a perfect letter of recommendation the LA cops wrote?"

I almost blushed, remembering it. "The chief may have gone a little overboard."

"The chief was 100 percent accurate, honey."

Made in the USA
Monee, IL
29 August 2020